R

"You'd Fit In With The Tallchiefs Perfectly,

"if you'd put out one little bit of effort," Michelle said. "I won't go away until I have answers, you know."

"What would you know of fitting in?" Liam asked too sharply, resenting the anger and frustration this woman could jerk from him. "You think you fit into this small town? You think you fit into my son's life? You think you can push and shove and place people in neat little boxes and everything will be just fine?"

"Friday night, the Tallchiefs are having a party. Be there. It's time you got to know them."

She marched out of his house and slammed the door behind her. His instincts told him to capture that hot-tempered, pride-filled witch, to claim that soft mouth, to fill his hands with her hair and keep her close until she—

The woman was pure trouble. Trouble that he didn't need....

Dear Reader,

Silhouette is celebrating our 20ᵗʰ anniversary in 2000, and the latest powerful, passionate, provocative love stories from Silhouette Desire are as hot as that steamy summer weather!

For August's MAN OF THE MONTH, the fabulous BJ James begins her brand-new miniseries, MEN OF BELLE TERRE. In *The Return of Adams Cade*, a self-made millionaire returns home to find redemption in the arms of his first love.

Beloved author Cait London delivers another knockout in THE TALLCHIEFS miniseries with *Tallchief: The Homecoming*, also part of the highly sensual Desire promotion BODY & SOUL. And Desire is proud to present *Bride of Fortune* by Leanne Banks, the launch title of FORTUNE'S CHILDREN: THE GROOMS, another exciting spin-off of the bestselling Silhouette FORTUNE'S CHILDREN continuity miniseries.

BACHELOR BATTALION marches on with Maureen Child's *The Last Santini Virgin,* in which a military man's passion for a feisty virgin weakens his resolve not to marry. *In Name Only* is how a sexy rodeo cowboy agrees to temporarily wed a pregnant preacher's daughter in the second book of Peggy Moreland's miniseries TEXAS GROOMS. And Christy Lockhart reconciles a once-married couple who are stranded together in a wintry cabin during *One Snowbound Weekend.…*

So indulge yourself by purchasing all six of these summer delights from Silhouette Desire…and read them in air-conditioned comfort.

Enjoy!

Joan Marlow Golan

Joan Marlow Golan
Senior Editor, Silhouette Desire

Please address questions and book requests to:
Silhouette Reader Service
U.S.: 3010 Walden Ave., P.O. Box 1325, Buffalo, NY 14269
Canadian: P.O. Box 609, Fort Erie, Ont. L2A 5X3

Cait London

TALLCHIEF: THE HOMECOMING

Published by Silhouette Books

America's Publisher of Contemporary Romance

To my readers
who have enjoyed the Cait London Tallchief series
and asked for more.

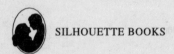 SILHOUETTE BOOKS

ISBN 0-373-76310-7

TALLCHIEF: THE HOMECOMING

Copyright © 2000 by Lois Kleinsasser

Visit Silhouette at www.eHarlequin.com

Printed in U.S.A.

CAIT LONDON

lives in the Missouri Ozarks but loves to travel the Northwest's gold rush/cattle drive trails every summer. She enjoys going on research trips, meeting people and going to Native American dances. Ms. London is an avid reader who loves to paint, play with computers and grow herbs (particularly scented geraniums right now). She's a national bestselling and award-winning author, and she has also written historical romances under another pseudonym. Three is her lucky number; she has three daughters, and the events in her life have always been in threes. "I love writing for Silhouette," Cait says. "One of the best perks about all this hard work is the thrilling reader response and the warm, snug sense that I have given readers an enjoyable, entertaining gift."

FAMILY TREE

Tallchief and Una Fearghus
(A Sioux chieftain captures a Scots bondwoman, who tames him.) 5 children

Liam and Elizabeth Montclair
(As a virgin, the English lady would inherit an empire; to save her sister from torture, she takes an unwilling staked-out half-breed. Out for revenge, he finds love.) 3 children

Ewan and Josette Tallchief
(Her Alaskan salmon fishing boat wrecked, fiery Josette must depend on a man she detests, Ewan. Her husband of convenience doesn't make her life easy.) 3 children

Jamie and Tina Tallchief
(Whimsy store owner Tina isn't prepared for a rough woodsman with a criminal record. When she's in danger, he kidnaps her for a dogsled ride that ends in a secluded cabin.) 2 children

Adam   Liam

Legends of the Tallchiefs

Liam—When a man and a woman, equally matched, strike against each other, fire will fly—just as two flints striking sparks off each other.

THE FLINT AND THE FIRE

"When a man and a woman, equally matched, strike against each other, fire will fly—just as two flints striking sparks off each other. 'Tis a game, finding the strength of a man and challenging that truth. I am a woman used to having my way, and being captured by a man who had fathered my child was no easy matter. How I battled with him, that great hard man, Liam Tallchief, scarred with life. He did not yield to me, nor would I have him be less than he was. But in the end, he filled my heart and a softness grew between us. I knew no other would make me feel so alive. No other could take my heart as Liam Tallchief. When he held our son, and that gentleness came upon him, I knew— I claimed him with a ring, and marked him for my own. For his part, he gave me two flints, the tinderbox marked with the Tallchief symbol, and a love that burns true."

—Elizabeth Tallchief

Prologue

Please forgive me, I should have told you that you were a stolen baby, but I couldn't.

The paper in Liam's trembling hand rattled, the woman's dainty handwriting blurring before his eyes, "Liam" the envelope had read, tucked into the pages of Mary Cartwright's beloved Bible. Mary had died when Liam was only six, and the years after her death had been sheer hell. Reuben—her husband—had little patience for a child, and Liam's life had consisted of scrambling for food and clothing. He'd been far too young for the long hours worked at Reuben's gas station.

Liam was a man now, at thirty-four, sorting possessions after Reuben's funeral. Hard and bullying Reuben had outlived Mary, as well as Liam's wife, who had passed away in childbirth.

Liam swallowed, the memory of his wife, Karen, tugging at his heart. Mary would have loved Karen, both sweet and loving women. Liam scrubbed his hand across his forehead, damning himself again for yielding to her plea for a baby: his son's birth had taken Karen's life.

The small cluttered apartment behind the gas station offered little comfort for a man in the lonely hours of a Wyoming night. Liam's hand curled around his son's small plastic truck—a reminder that life went on and was good, and children could be raised by a single father and be well loved. "J.T.," Jacob Thomas, was only two and sleeping quietly while Liam dealt with the past. Liam studied his hand—big and scarred and darkly tanned, a workman's hand holding a delicate paper that he sensed would rip away his life. The mirror in the shadows reflected a harsh face, high cheekbones, searing gray eyes, a set jaw and a shaggy cut of thick, black hair—a contrast to Mary's and Reuben's fair complexions. As a young man, Liam had towered over Reuben's stocky build, and the abuse had stopped.

Liam listened as J.T. sighed in his sleep, then returned to the letter Mary had hidden in a place Reuben would never look—the Bible. The letter to Liam had waited for years, and he braced himself to continue reading....

My own baby was stillborn that night, a little son with blond curls. Reuben had been drinking heavily, yelling at me for my failure. I'd lost babies before, and Reuben had no son, which he thought made his mark as a man. There was no doctor. Reuben said we couldn't afford one for "women's work." I took drugs to escape the pain and Reuben's fury and held my baby close for comfort. I remember that night, the way the lightning seared the windows, the thunder crashing. Reuben was muttering then, holding his whisky and staring out into the night. He said they were fools, whoever was driving across the mountain river, he'd make them pay a flat fee for pulling them out with his wrecker.

Liam inhaled slowly, his hands shaking as he read Mary's letter: *Then he was back, dripping with rain and taking away my baby, replacing him with you. "Let them think he's dead," Reuben said. I wept horribly. Then you nudged my breast, and milk dampened my nightgown and I took you for my own, loving you instantly. I guessed your age then to be about two weeks. We waited two more before asking a doctor to examine you and produce a birth certificate.*

I knew it was wrong, but I wanted you more than my life. Reuben had said the car had crashed in to the river and there were no surviors, just you, and now you were his—and mine—a son at last. How selfish I was, wanting the baby suckling at my breast, cuddling you against the ache in my heart. "Liam" was embroidered upon your sleepers, and I insisted on that for your name. Reuben has forgotten the chest that was found with you, but it is hidden beneath the boards I cut in the bedroom floor. I have no reason to believe that Reuben will ever want a home away from here, or his gas station, so the chest will be safe. The sheriff investigating the accident said your parents were drowned, washed away in the torrent after their car went into the river. Their bodies were found, and the baby presumed dead. But I held you tightly and was silent, fearing they would take you away.

"Their names were Tallchief, Liam. Your name is Liam Tallchief, not Cartwright. I love you. Forgive me. Mary."

One

One year later—

Liam Tallchief wasn't in the mood for the classy woman on his doorstep. The commanding tone to her slightly husky voice reminded him of Reuben's bullish demands.

A year ago, Liam had torn Reuben Cartwright's name from him; he'd taken his rightful name—Tallchief—for himself and his three-year-old son, and no one was ordering him around again…especially not a woman a foot shorter than his six-foot four-height.

She looked at her gold wristwatch, an expensive bangle style that slid on her slender wrist, and the myriad flash of her diamond ring hit his face. She glanced meaningfully up at him, impatient to have him tend her needs. Appearing to be in her early thirties, the woman was used to giving orders—and Liam didn't like taking them. She hadn't liked that his service station was closed, but then, at seven o'clock in the evening, the residents of Amen Flats, Wyoming were settling into their homes, escaping the late-July heat. Liam recognized the expression of a person used to commanding others, and he didn't like it.

At thirty-five, Liam knew his priorities: The green-eyed woman with a heart-shaped face could wait; his son's needs came first.

"My son is eating now. When he's finished we'll go and get your car. Or you can use my phone to call anyone you like," Liam said coolly. He'd grown up with people knocking on his door, asking for towing help with that hot, frustrated look. Back then, Reuben didn't care if the son he had stolen was fed and warm.

Son. A momentary darkness shrouded Liam, the recent discovery of his birthright still raw. As a two-week-old infant, he'd taken a dead baby's place in Mary's loving arms. His name was Tallchief now, not Cartwright.

The woman's restless stance, her hand brushing her hair back from her face, nettled Liam. Perhaps the summer thunderstorm brewing high on Tallchief Mountain that caused him to brood...perhaps it was the woman, looking as if she had everything and wanting more.

"I saw your note on the station door, to come here— the house behind the station. I'm trying to surprise a friend, not ask them to come fetch me. I suppose you have the only towing service in town," the woman said as she stood in the doorway of his rented house. She scanned the main street of Amen Flats, Wyoming, the sunlight glistening on her blond hair and highlighting the dark-brown of her brows and her lashes. "I'd rather no one saw me like this."

He caught the expensive flash of tiny, bold earrings and the phrase *no one,* and tossed the term aside; the wealthy often dismissed those who served their needs into the "no one" bin. The tiny town nestled at the foot of the mountains wouldn't call to her, a city woman, as it did to Liam.

For it was in Amen Flats that he sensed he would find peace, where he had to make peace for his son's sake. A man who had been raised in one identity only to discover his life had been a lie, Liam had done his share of brooding. He'd changed his name to Tallchief and he'd moved here, to try to do his best. He'd missed a heritage, and for Jacob Thomas, "J.T.," Liam would try to learn about his family.

"You don't say much, do you?" Standing in the doorway of his rented house, the woman shifted impatiently from the foot clad in torn hose to the one in an expensive gray heel. The rap-rap of her hand against her costly, overstuffed shoulder tote said she wasn't used to waiting, her diamonds glittering in the late July sunset. Heat had flushed her face, darkening the strands of blond hair on her cheek. The waves rippled tightly, impatiently propped onto the top of her head with an office rubber band. The plain rubber band contrasted the long, lean expensive line of her gray pinstripe suit jacket and skirt. The diamond solitaire nestled at her throat cost more than his tow truck, but J.T.'s evening meal was more important than a rich woman's impatience.

"Daddy?" At Liam's side, J.T. wrapped his arm around his father's leg; his other hand caught the loop fashioned on his father's loose denim pants. Dressed in a T-shirt and cutoff jean shorts, J.T.'s gray eyes widened fearfully up at the woman. J.T. had seen enough of suit-clad women who had come to take him away from his father, "for better care."

No one was taking Liam's son from him. He'd had

enough of people prying into his business when his wife died and J.T. was just a baby.

The woman glanced quickly from father to son. "You look just alike. Scowlers, both of you."

"You're not exactly smiling yourself. It's okay, Son. Finish your supper," Liam said, rubbing the top of his son's glossy black hair. J.T. often needed reassurance, and Liam knew how it felt to be young and frightened— only Reuben had been short on tender, loving care.

Liam pushed back that quiver of hatred snaking through him. He glanced at the dark clouds topping Tallchief Mountain. *Less than a year before, Liam had learned that he wasn't Reuben's son, but that his rightful name was Tallchief—that he was the missing baby of the deceased Tallchief couple swept away in the river, after their car wreck. His entire life had been a lie...his son would have the truth.*

"It's a little late for him to be eating, isn't it?" the woman asked, and blew a long rippling strand away from her face. Sunset caught sparks in blond hair and formed a halo of rippling wisps around her head; the woman's hair was naturally curly and most likely unable to be tamed.

"Could be," Liam answered, in the way that he knew avoided more questions. Earlier J.T. had been napping so peacefully on his little cot at the station that Liam was able to finish a tune-up job. He set his most intricate work around the boy's sleep and play patterns. "You're welcome to come in."

"Do you have air-conditioning?" she asked, as if setting contract terms, and pushed up her suit's long sleeve to study her watch. Her nose wrinkled distastefully as she glanced down to her torn hose and wiggled her toes. "I hate being dirty and sweaty," she stated adamantly.

"You look like a Tallchief. My friend Silver Tallchief Palladin sent a picture of the family to me...they're quite impressive all decked out in kilts and tartans. It's easy to see you're related somehow. Silver is a cousin. Her husband is a Palladin and a brother to the man who married Fiona."

She'd come to his doorstep, demanding help, and without knowing it, had slapped him with his problems. With shaggy black hair and smoky-gray eyes, Liam was a perfect reflection of the Amen Flats Tallchiefs, but he preferred to keep to himself. Reuben had taught him that— that a shroud of cool distance was safer than family. The extensive Tallchief family hadn't pushed, but Liam hadn't offered, either. He wasn't certain how he fit into the Tallchief bloodline, but he knew after one look at Duncan, Calum, Birk, Fiona and Elspeth that he was related.

He intended J.T. to know who he was, where he came from, and to have a family. The problem was that Liam didn't know how to enter a family—

After Reuben died, Liam was left with medical bills and the job of cleaning up old papers. There, in Mary Cartwright's Bible, had been a small perfect letter for "My Son Liam." *And then he had learned how Reuben had substituted an orphaned baby for his own stillborn son.*

Thunder rumbled on Tallchief Mountain, and the waves on Tallchief Lake would be lashed with whitecaps, the wind damp with rain. Mary, Liam's foster mother, had been kind, but had passed away soon after Liam's sixth birthday. Next, sweet Karen, Liam's wife, had passed silently away after bearing J.T. And then old Reuben—Liam swallowed the tight hatred in his throat—the man who had picked him up from the river bank was tight with money, bitter with words and fast to use his hands on a child. But not on J.T.; Reuben had known better than to touch Liam's son as he had hurt Liam.

Liam nodded, picking up J.T. in his arms and opening the door for the woman to enter his house. His son hooked an arm tightly around Liam's neck, and Liam held him closer. "It's all right, J.T.," he said quietly, and closed the door of his plain, clean house behind the woman.

She entered with quick assessing glances, taking in the bare furnishings, the toys and trucks strewn across the floor, the shabby desk piled high with papers and bills. She frowned at the clutter of a disassembled carburetor on a side table—Liam's work while J.T. slept. "I'll wait here," she said, sitting very straight in a battered chair. She clasped her huge leather, business bag on her lap as she glanced at her watch yet again.

Liam tossed aside the deliberate, impatient nudge. "If you want, you can use the bathroom to freshen up."

Her body tightened within the fluid expensive suit, and he almost smiled at her distaste. While his towels and bathroom were meticulous—a contrast to the filth in which he'd grown up—there were no hand creams or special tissues available. "No, thank you. I'm just fine," she said.

She stirred restlessly, and while he sat with J.T., he noted her obvious reluctance to change her mind. "Well, maybe I should just freshen up while you finish," she said, holding her heavy shoulder bag tightly as she entered the bathroom. Her wary expression said she didn't trust him.

Liam ate quietly, helping J.T. with his spoon and using a paper napkin to set an example. He knew little about trust, except his son's.

When she came out, J.T. sniffed at the delicate flower scent, an oddity in the all male house. The little boy's eyes widened as she produced a tube of hand cream and began working it into her hands. He sniffed again, unfamiliar with the feminine action. J.T. finished his chicken take-out meal, his gray eyes wary on the woman. Her eyes were as green as summer grass when Liam served her ice water. "Thank you very much," she said very properly, and sipped the water. Then she was up on her feet, pacing in an odd, one-heeled way, a restless woman ready to be off and tearing through life. Liam recognized the type, well dressed, raised in a life of money, eager for more money, and little time for anything in between.

Breeding and money, Liam thought, as she handed the glass back to him. The diamond studs in those dainty ears cost enough to clothe J.T. for years. When J.T. was finished, Liam told him to get ready, and the boy solemnly went to the bathroom. He appeared moments later with his favorite red ball cap and toy truck, standing close to Liam.

After handing J.T. into the wrecker and buckling him into his car seat, Liam turned to help the woman up into the seat. Several feet off the ground, the high cab required the use of a handgrip and a running board. She hitched up her skirt with one hand and stepped onto the metal running board with her unshod foot. It was dainty, Liam noticed absently, small and narrow and perfect within the ruined, dirty hose. From the severe way she dressed, he wasn't expecting the neatly lacquered dark-red toenails. She gripped the pipe handle on the side of the truck, and pulled herself up to the running board, balancing precariously.

In the next moment her high heel caught, and she twisted, tumbling back into Liam's arms.

He hadn't had a woman in his arms for years. The stunning softness of her hips and the softness of her breasts beneath his fingers shocked him. One glance down to her slightly parted suit jacket and the glimpse of quivering golden flesh took away his breath.

"Sorry," she said, scowling up at him as the sensual vibrations held him trapped.

"Maybe you'd better take off your shoe—so it won't cause you to fall again," he offered roughly when he could catch his breath.

"Just look at my hose," she said accusingly, as if he were the cause. She stretched out a neatly curved leg and pointed her toe. "If you think I'm going to let that happen, think again," she stated, clearly offended.

Liam nodded and tried to focus on what he was supposed to be doing, but all he could think about was the soft, sweet-smelling woman in his arms and those stormy green eyes. *Witch's eyes filled with secrets and brewing enough heat to scorch him....*

Expensive. Spoiled. High-class. The thoughts rapped at him as he managed to place her back on the running board. She tottered precariously, and Liam shook his head and closed his eyes momentarily. Then he placed a broad hand on her backside and pushed her upward. She lifted her skirt again, and from below Liam was presented with a mind-blowing view of long legs up to her thighs, and a neatly curved bottom. He blinked, trying to force away the image of a beige-pink lacy slip.

He blinked again, for the beige-pink lace matched the lace that had been exposed by her gaping suit jacket.

Liam suddenly realized that it was very hot in the late

July sunset, and that he was feeling unstable and meltable.

"I'm ready," she said imperially from feet above him, the queen to the servant. She met his look evenly. "You can stop scowling now."

He slammed the door on her snooty tone and the intriguing view of her slender, curved legs.

He was just recovering, shifting gears and driving down the highway when she looked at him over J.T.'s head. "He doesn't say much, and neither do you."

She'd torn through his attempt at reclaiming silence and peace. The woman irritated and pushed, Liam thought doggedly. He didn't like feeling nettled. "He's fine."

But J.T. was frightened, his little hand reaching out to grip Liam's T-shirt. That small, tight fist sent a bolt of pain to Liam's heart. As a boy, he'd known about fear, and he didn't want J.T. frightened. Liam didn't know how to share the boy, how to make him feel safe with others. He hoped that eventually J.T. would learn to trust others, because if anything happened to Liam, J.T. would be alone—

"You shouldn't have brought him. He could get hurt. Couldn't you have called a baby-sitter?"

"No." Liam knew his answer was too harsh. But until J.T. settled in better—

"I would have thought any of the Tallchiefs—"

"We don't mix much." Liam watched a doe and fawn cross the highway, pointing to the animals for J.T.'s pleasure. Until six months ago, J.T. had grown up in Moss, a small Wyoming mountain town. Deer were plentiful near Moss and had always fascinated J.T.

"His mother, then." The woman's slanted green eyes

flashed in the shadows; she was a fighter, determined to make her point.

Liam resented the need to answer, but she wasn't the kind to let be. "We're alone."

The woman was checking her watch again, distracted by her misfortune. "I don't have time for this."

She rubbed her upper stomach in a gesture that Liam knew—the woman probably had an ulcer. But it wasn't enough to distract her from him— "The Tallchief family is supposed to be very close. All that heritage thing going for them—kilts and Native American."

"I wouldn't know much about that."

"You should. Your son deserves to know all he can about his heritage."

"That's our business," Liam said too quietly, in a raised-hackles, hands-off tone that most people recognized. He'd heard about the Tallchief legend of how a Sioux chieftain captured a Scots bondwoman and how she tamed him. He'd heard of the contemporary Tallchiefs, how they dressed in kilts and tartans at family gatherings. He wanted J.T. to know about who he was, where he came from, but Liam didn't know how to be a part of a family. He'd tried for his wife's sake, and loving him, Karen had understood. He didn't like being pushed; he'd had enough from old Reuben.

She sat straighter, her lips tightening, clearly wanting to say more. One darting glance at J.T. told Liam that, if not for his child, she would be tearing into him. Those green eyes flashed at him through the shadowy cab of the tow truck. Then she checked her watch again, eager to be away from a man who didn't take good care of his child. Her slight sniff and the way she set her jaw said more than words.

That grated. So did the soft scent filling his cab, tantalizing over the grease odor and J.T.'s recent boat and bubble bath.

Shifting restlessly in the cab, she ripped a cellular phone from the big business bag. "Eight o'clock in Wyoming. Amen Flats. I'm here. My car is dead, and I'm not happy. I paid a mint for it, and it's sitting out here in the wilderness steaming like a boiling crab pot. I'll call when I'm at Silver's. Make certain that memo to Charleston Presents goes out in the morning. And a mass mailing out to all the applicants for the new opening. I worked overtime getting the text just right on the screening test. When those tests come back, create a file for each one. I'll go over them when I get back. And have Hazel run a comparison of insurance health benefits and of the funds in our employees' retirement packages. No, don't call me. I'll check in. I don't want my friend's household disturbed by my business. And see if you can send an extra supply of my favorite hosiery.... *What? Again?*"

When she punched off the cell phone, she sat back against the seat, her elegant hands locked in a white-knuckled grip upon her thick tote-bag. As if remembering something, she tore into the bag, rummaged and came out with an envelope. Her hands were shaking as she opened the letter, scanning it.

Liam concentrated on the winding mountain road. Her problems weren't his, and he kept to his own life, he told himself as she placed the letter in the envelope and then in the bag too precisely, as if she were filing it away. He recognized her tight, closed expression; the woman wasn't sharing her problems, and he wasn't asking.

J.T. watched with fascination as she rummaged in the big tote again, produced a laptop computer and braced it on her thighs. After a moment of frowning and tsking and punching keys, she clicked it closed, replaced it in her tote and folded her arms over her chest. "My car is just around that bend."

The silver luxury car was missing a part that would take days to replace, refusing to start. Liam pointed to a safe spot, and J.T. moved to stand quietly aside. "Starter," Liam said, and J.T. nodded. When Liam finished attaching the car to the tow truck, J.T. stood beside him. J.T.'s small hands hooked into his cutoff pockets the same as Liam had hooked into his carpenter pants. He wore the carpenter pants for a reason—if his hands were busy at the grocery store or when paying a bill, J.T. was to grip the loop for the hammer and stay close. As a single father he'd discovered many ways to keep close watch on his son.

The woman blew a tendril of silky hair away from her nose. "He acts like you, right down to those fierce, scowling looks when he thinks I'm picking on you. Clearly he's protective of you. You haven't asked, but my name is Michelle Farrell. You'll need my name for the bill. You don't ask questions, do you? In fact, you don't talk much at all. You need to talk more to your son, not just gesture and point when you want him to do something. Are you certain you know about attaching my car to your truck? You won't break or dent anything?"

Liam had had enough. He usually shed comments like hers, but there was something about the woman that grated. "Do you have kids?" he asked abruptly.

Clearly startled, she blinked up at him. "Well, no. I was married, but I…I opted for a career, not children."

"Well, then. I guess I'm more experienced at child care, aren't I," he stated—it wasn't a question—and then picked her up and sat her on the fender of his wrecker. The slender indentation of her waist burned his hands long after he released her. "Stay put and out of the way. At least my son knows when not to talk and to stay out of danger."

He turned away and wondered at the tiny rivulet of pleasure running through him. He wasn't that accustomed to pleasure, other than enjoying J.T., but Michelle's startled expression was a definite payoff after her pushing. She quickly adjusted to the situation, looking very much like the queen overlooking her servant as he worked.

Her long, crossed legs, one dainty foot in torn hose and the other clad in an expensive shoe, were hard to ignore. The slight rain began and, used to taking care of his son's needs first, Liam lifted J.T. into the cab, strapping him into his car seat. Then because the boy looked uncertain, fearing that the woman would ask him prying questions, Liam kissed him and nuzzled his throat, making bear noises.

Through the window he spotted Michelle glaring at him. She'd taken off the rubber band, and her hair caught the mist, the rippling waves floating around her shoulders and lifting in the slight wind. The strands whirled gently around her, fascinating him for just a heartbeat. He sensed she wouldn't ask for help—women like her were used to being cared for—and with a doomed sigh he went to lift her down from the fender.

Michelle scowled down at the man who had briskly, efficiently detached her car at his service station, as if he'd like to be freed of her as well. He'd driven her to Silver and Nick's country home with only the sound of the windshield wipers slashing and the child stirring restlessly between them. He'd torn open the door, leaped to the ground, and now he jerked open her door and waited for her.

Liam Tallchief was gorgeous, standing in the rain, his T-shirt plastered to his broad chest, his long legs spread wide and clad in loose carpenter pants, his worn biker's boots braced on the paved driveway.

She eased J.T.'s head from her shoulder, and with a sigh, the child slept deeply. His raven hair and lashes an exact match to his father's. The adorable child was one matter, his father another. She hadn't liked Liam from the moment he'd opened his house door. He'd been too brooding, too silent, and his dark, fierce expression— those stormy gray eyes narrowing at her between his long, black glossy lashes... Or maybe it was the lock of his jaw, his set mouth that set her nerves humming.

"Coming?" he asked in a slow, deep voice with just the touch of insolence to set her off.

"If I find one dent—"

"Uh-huh. You'll sue."

"If I ran Dover's human resources branch like you run your business—"

"Uh-huh. Does all that hair get wild and curly as sunlit witch's silk when you get mad?"

Sunlit witch's silk. The romantic image knocked the air from her. She moved her lips, and nothing would come out. She blinked when he ordered, "Jump. I'll catch you. That's a whole lot easier than you falling into my arms."

Michelle's thoughts ran across her mind like a digital printout: she ran an office staff of twenty-five people; she organized conferences, testing and training programs, dealt with personnel problems and issued reports. An expert profiler, she drew an ungodly salary, and this service station hero was insinuating that she was a *klutz?* Taking a deep breath, Michelle prepared to tell him off.

His black hair gleamed with rain as he tilted his head

to one side, studying her. She tried with dignity to work her way out of the cab, her shoe slipped on the wet running board and she tumbled into his arms. "Uh!"

He held her tight against him, looking down at her through the heavy rain as though she were a prize he could carry off. The cool damp air quivered between them, and the strong shoulder she had grabbed as she fell flexed beneath her palm. Liam's gray eyes slowly ran down her body, paused at the crevice of her breasts, nestled in her gray suit jacket, and he trembled, holding her tighter.

There in the slashing rain, he was like no other man she'd ever known—his skin gleaming damply, his cheekbones harsh and his jaw unrelenting. She dug her fingers deeper, wanting to keep this fierce man close, to study him, to feel that raw, stormy essence—

A real man, she thought, *no pretense, just the thin veneer of civilization.* He could have been a warrior carrying off a bride as Tallchief had carried Una Fearghus—Michelle shivered and licked the raindrop from her lip, and his gray eyes seared her mouth. She sucked in air, catching the scent of rain and of man and a mystery that she had to unravel. Liam Tallchief's expression darkened as the wind whipped her hair around her, a strand clinging to his cheek.

The fierce, elemental storm circling them seemed meek when compared to the electricity leaping between them as gray eyes locked with dark green—

"Michelle!" Silver's voice startled her, breaking the spell, and Liam tensed. Then in the next moment he was running through the rain, carrying her to the Palladins' front porch. He returned to the tow truck, extracted her two large designer suitcases from the back and ran through the rain, carrying them easily.

She had just finished hugging Silver and was preparing to tell him off, when he grinned and knocked away her breath. "She's mad as a wet hen," he said to Silver, and reached to stroke away a strand of hair from Michelle's cheek.

Then he frowned briefly, quickly turning and hurrying back to his sleeping son…and leaving her heart pounding wildly, inexplicably.

"Okay, let's have it. You usually handle unexpected situations easily. You're very capable. It isn't the car breaking down, is it? It's something to do with Liam Tallchief," Silver said as Michelle stalked the length of the guest room, dressed in black satin pajamas. Nick and Silver's three-month-old daughter, Jasmine, was asleep in her crib, and Nick was washing the dishes and settling the house. A basket of diapers sat on Michelle's bed, waiting for Silver to fold them.

"Liam Tallchief is rude, brooding, evil and despicable. He's overbearing, too macho, and when he does manage to talk, he orders. I cannot stand arrogant men. More than likely he expects women to wait on him and fall at his feet, obeying his every whim."

"Oh, is that all?" Silver asked with amusement and sprawled on the quilt, grinning, her head propped in her hand and looking ready for girl talk. A nursing mother, Silver's body was ripe and curved and she was clearly in love with Nick, who adored her. A professional perfumer who once had white-blond hair, Silver's hair was now gleaming black, fashioned into two long braids.

"I'm going to investigate him. I've handled enough personnel records to know that he's hiding something. He's wearing a big Hands Off sign."

"Can't help you much. He came here about six months

ago and leased that service station from George Myers. George's wife wanted to travel in their senior years, and Liam drove that wrecker into town with J.T. sitting right next to him. One look at Liam and J.T. and you know they're related to the Tallchiefs. The whole family is one to respect privacy and they are not asking questions. It's enough for them that he's here. When J.T. isn't feeling well, Liam closes the station and stays with him. They seem so alone. Liam always finds some excuse to avoid coming to Tallchief House and has little to say to the family. We keep inviting him, and he keeps turning us down. Elspeth seems awfully quiet when his name comes up, and that usually means something is afoot that she doesn't want to share. One thing is for certain—Liam is totally dedicated to J.T.''

Michelle folded her arms over her chest. ''He refused to work on my car. He said I'd have to have it towed to the next town, to the dealer licensed to make repairs.... Why wouldn't he want to visit a family as obviously loving and close as the Tallchiefs? Why wouldn't he want J.T. to play with children his own age?'' *Why did he hold her as if nothing could take her away, as if she were rightfully his?*

Why did her body tremble against him? Why did she feel a fierce urge to claim him? The unexpected softness within her, the need to place her hand along his cheek and soothe him couldn't be explained.

She was highly educated, a competent businesswoman with career goals. She didn't function on basic instincts, rather filtering knowledge as she was trained to do. Liam Tallchief raised raw edges in her smoothly honed personality, and she didn't like being aware of him as a man.

Who was he? Who was she?

Michelle ran her hands through her hair, smoothing it.

She sensed his need to grip her hair, to fill his fists with it. *Why?*

She decided to blame her unsteady, stormy emotions on the night, on her mishap, on an overpriced car that hissed steam at her, on the long walk into town with a broken heel.

She ran her hands over her face. She'd been divorced for two years, and perhaps in her heart she was never really married. She didn't have the natural urges to have children, but J.T. made her want to cuddle him.

"These small-town mechanics think they're gods with special rights. He thinks he can push me around—well, he can't. I'm going down to that station tomorrow and—"

"Liam Tallchief doesn't seem like a man who likes being pushed," Silver noted with a delighted grin. "He's got to you, hasn't he? You never could stand a good mystery…you always wanted everything in black-and-white and instantly. He's got the patience to finish a crossword puzzle. You don't."

Michelle threw a pillow at Silver. "It's your fault for making country life sound so simple. I could be in my nice penthouse now in Seattle. But oh, no—'Come see the baby,' you said. How could I refuse to see Jasmine, the most beautiful and intelligent baby in all the galaxies?"

Silver smiled softly, and when she took away the pillow she'd been hugging against her, two dark, damp spots showed on her blouse. "I love being a wife and mother. I didn't ever think I'd find peace after my sister passed away, but I did. The legend of the pearls was really true. Una, the Tallchiefs' Scots ancestor, had to sell her dowry to pay for Tallchief land. The Tallchiefs of Amen Flats lost their parents when the oldest child was only eighteen, and they decided to reclaim Una's dowry. A legend is attached to each dowry item. Elizabeth Montclair, an Englishwoman, married Una and Tallchief's son. His name was Liam, too. Elizabeth left the legend of the pearls... 'If he places them upon her, warmed by his flesh, and gives her a sweet kiss, the pearls will be her undoing.' They really were my undoing. I found myself here with the Tallchiefs, and if Liam will open his heart, he'll find peace, too. He just doesn't know how, yet, and he's fighting the past, just like I did.''

Her voice was soft now as Michelle came to sit by her. Silver studied her friend. ''I want you to have what I've found. You're strained...I can tell by the circles under your eyes, and you're very pale as if nothing has given you peace for years. I know that haunted look. Before I met Nick, I tried to push away my problems, and bury them with work. You're running too fast, honey. Slow down and enjoy life here—while you're here.''

''I'm still at odds with my parents. Mother is pushing me to reconcile with Dad before too much more time passes. That's not likely to happen. He hasn't forgiven me for not entering business with him. They were against my divorce, wanting me to stay in a life that neither Oliver nor I wanted. Oliver was like a son to Dad, and all the pretty picture lacked was me—what I wanted. I wanted a career, and they wanted a business wife. Dad and Oliver thought I'd change my mind after the marriage—I had to fight both of them.''

Michelle shrugged. ''You've done what you wanted—started a top perfume business. I like taking care of peoples' lives—their retirement, health care, promotions. I'm good at what I do, fitting people into places they belong. I could fit Liam into the Tallchief family, if I wanted.''

''Such confidence. I'd almost bet you on that. Liam

isn't going to be fitted into anything until he's ready."
Silver began to fold the diapers in the laundry basket.
"You like structure. Liam Tallchief runs on instincts, and
he isn't a man to push, or to let someone else take charge
of his life. I was an outsider here once, too, and I recognize that look in Liam."

"Whatever. I'm not much for legends, even Tallchief
lore, though they are romantic. I deal in realities. All of
you are letting Liam Tallchief have his way. He can't
keep that beautiful child to himself forever. You said he
hasn't visited any of you."

"He's picking his time. One look at him and you just
know that he's been terribly wounded and that he's just
coping the best he can. None of us would take that away
from him."

"I'm not certain that he deserves any courtesies. He's
a very…uncivilized man, but I'm betting I can do the
job—fitting him into the Tallchiefs, for his son's sake, if
not for his. I'll just take your bet and up the ante—he'll
be in that family within two weeks or I'll do every one
of Jasmine's diapers in the last week I'm here." Michelle
studied the bolt of lightning outside the house. She'd run
all her life, pushing for multiple college degrees, for a
high salary job, for the perfect wedding, the perfect marriage, a stuffed bank account— Who was she? And where
was she going?

Why, out there in the rain, had Liam Tallchief held
her as if they were nothing but a man and a woman?

She tried to sleep later, her body exhausted but her
mind running on, filled with Liam's dark, possessive expression, the sudden clench of his body searing hers in
the cold summer rain. *Sunlit witch's silk,* he'd said,
haunting her as the storm crashed around the Palladin
ranch.

A practical woman, the romantic phrase snared her—
Sunlit witch's silk.

Then she awoke, cold and sweating, a silent scream
locked in her throat. The tender phrase had turned and
curled around her like soft ribbons. Then with a hard tug,
it flipped to a nightmare and another's man's voice and
a coarse, *Witch. I'll get you for this. You should have
kept quiet and now you're going to pay.* From the shadows of the twisted nightmare, the man's expression was
maniacal. Theron Oswald held a knife at her throat and
damned her for exposing his past in the employment
background check—

Michelle scrubbed her hands over her face, pushing
away the lurking nightmare. She'd given the police all
the information she could on the man stalking her, and
yet he'd eluded them. When her secretary told her of a
threatening call from a pay phone, she'd reread Theron's
letter in the wrecker. "I'll get you for this...."

Michelle shuddered briefly, then she thought of another
man—one with a hard face and smoky gray eyes and
wild, windswept black hair. She thought of him laughing
up at her, challenging her to leap to him from his
wrecker. Suddenly, she wasn't cold anymore, her temper
rising as she planned on how to deal with him.

Two

"**B**ackground checks. I'm good at them. You failed, Tallchief," Michelle stated crisply. The rhythmic sound of paper slapped against flesh drew Liam's eyes up to the long, tanned, bare legs above him. Liam's palm ached to slide up that smooth length— Only one woman in Amen would wear a diamond ankle chain with her expensive running shoes. The ankle chain matched the simple diamond bracelet on her wrist. Michelle Farrell's legs looked even more enticing than the night before, sheathed in a wet skirt, torn nylons and one shoe. From the pit beneath the car, where he had been changing oil and installing a new muffler in Lyle Eubank's old pickup, he watched the high-priced running shoe tap on the service station's not-so-clean cement floor. Liam glanced at J.T., who was sleeping on his cot, cuddling his favorite toy truck; he didn't want his son to hear an argument with the woman poking through his past.

Liam usually stopped what he was doing immediately to wait on customers, but the Farrell woman could set him off. He continued to work, tightening the brackets for the new muffler. She could unnerve him, he brooded, and twisted a bolt too tight. He preferred the shadows, not the gleam of rain dancing on warm, soft lips. He knew the shadows, walked in them, except for the moments he enjoyed his son. He couldn't trust that happy little zing shooting through him when Michelle ignited. In the rain last night those wide green eyes had devoured him, and her delicate fingers had gripped his shoulders. She was stronger than she looked, less fragile in his arms—more a willowy strength that could bend rather than break. That strand of silky, damp hair had locked him in place, tantalizing him; the soft nudge of her breast against his chest and the sight of her curves nestled against him had sent a white-hot jolt down to his lower belly.

He wasn't a sensual man. He'd loved his wife in a gentle way, careful of hurting her with his greater size. He'd brooded all night, unprepared for the instant, hard slam of lust. Other men spoke of it, but Liam had never experienced the hard rule of his body over his mind—until he'd had Michelle in his arms.

Her hurry-hurry, push-push made him want to slow her down, and there wasn't one reason he should want to taste those sassy lips, to grip her chin in his hand and take—

He tossed his wrench into the tool kit with his erotic thoughts about Michelle and methodically wiped his hands, taking his time before looking at her. He glanced unwillingly at those long, smooth legs above him and punched the lift button to raise the car on the rack. As it rose, Liam vaulted out of the pit easily and Michelle, suddenly startled, backed away, her backside hitting his work shelf.

Dressed in an expensive cream T-shirt and khaki shorts, a tiny gold chain around her slender throat, Michelle glared at him and wiped her bottom with her free hand. It came away smudged with grease and she looked at it in disdain. Her other hand held a rolled computer printout like a tightly gripped club. Propped high on top of her head, that fascinating blond hair seemed alive and glowing, shooting off sparks. Tendrils circled her face and spiraled down the back of her neck. The designer sunglasses perched on top of her head remained firmly in place as he suspected Michelle would tolerate nothing less.

Liam fought to suppress a smile as she brushed back a tendril of that fabulous, willful hair and left a dark smudge along her cheek. Clearly Michelle Farrell had never touched grease. A courteous man—as Liam usually was—would have shown her the heavy cleaning soap and given her a towel. This morning, with the Wyoming sun gleaming on his son's new tricycle outside the garage's repair bay, Liam didn't feel like giving her favors.

"An innocent man doesn't change his name, like you did a year ago," she launched at him.

She'd been prowling—a woman like her, tied to cellular phones and computers would want answers. He hadn't expected her determination or interest. Most people took note of his Hands Off signs, but then he hadn't exactly— The truth slammed into him: he'd locked her body to his, out there in the storm, and he'd wanted to carry her off.

Oil and water, he thought. Class and breeding were elements he didn't trust. A woman like Michelle was nothing but trouble. Her green eyes narrowed up at him

as she waited. Working for Reuben, Liam hadn't had
time for dating, until Karen in his last year of high
school. She was shy and sweet and he'd wanted to protect
her. It was a quiet loving and she soothed him, her softness filling the empty hole in his heart.

Michelle Farrell wasn't shy or sweet and needed no
one to protect her. She was spoiled, expensive and highly
volatile, and after his reaction to her, he intended to keep
his distance.

"I can tow your car to the franchised dealer for repair.
I'm not working on it," he said carefully. He wanted her
away from him, from his life. Michelle had dug in; she'd
probably ride his backside until the car was repaired, and
he didn't trust himself with her.

Those dark brown eyebrows lifted, her expression imperial. "You'd rather not work on my car. Isn't that
nice…a garage and a mechanic who can choose his customers."

"Yes, ma'am. But I didn't say *rather*. I said I'm not."
Liam took his time, preparing his thoughts and washing
the heavy grime from his hands. He dried very carefully,
aware that Michelle's grease-stained palm was still hovering, away from that taut curved body—the woman's
body he'd held in his arms last night, an unexpected sensual fever sweeping through him.

He'd wondered then, out there in the raging summer
storm, how that soft pale flesh would feel against his
darker skin—with nothing but rain between them. Pushing down an uncustomary curse, he slammed a drawer of
assorted bolts closed with unnecessary force.

"Why not? Why not work on my car?" Her sharp tone
told him that she wanted to take him apart—the lady
demanding and expecting her rights. She wouldn't take
less than her due.

"Don't want to," he said. He'd skipped the preliminaries, the warranty that would be invalidated if mechanics other than those trained in the high-priced brand worked on the car. He wished he hadn't turned—with just that jolt of excitement—to see if he could set her off....

"Well. How nice, Mr. Tallchief. I suppose you've got a waiting list, preferred customers and all that. You pump gas and order repair parts and once in a while hook your little wrecker and tow in a dead car. I don't see any exactly special or selective services in any of that. Just why don't I qualify as a customer?" Her dirty hand slashed the air, the wildly waving strands on the top of her head shimmering in the garage's shadowy light. The grease mark on her cheek gleamed against golden skin too soft for the scars and calluses of his hands.

"You can buy gas—when you've got a car that runs," he offered, wondering why he was enjoying the sight of this classy woman angry with him.

She glanced at J.T. to find him sleeping, before she tore into Liam, a courtesy he appreciated. She lowered her voice. "You've changed your name and your son's to Tallchief. I want to know why. You were born Liam Cartwright."

"It's my business." He hated the darkness from the past, the bitterness lashing at him. Mary, the woman he'd thought was his mother, had insisted on his name, linking him to his rightful inheritance—and he loved her for giving him that much. The judge who legally changed Liam and J.T.'s name understood his need to give his son more. No one else had a right to his past.

Liam wasn't ready to explore his past, shifting from one identity to another had been difficult enough. He knew himself well, and when he was ready, he would open the letters in the chest and face his past.

"No, I've made you my business. I won't let you hurt my friend or the family she loves. The Tallchiefs didn't question your motives—I do." The grease-stained hand reached to thrust against his chest, leaving the imprint of her small, graceful hand. Liam studied the black stain of a woman who wasn't likely to give up easily. He almost admired her, a woman who would fight for those she loved, but he couldn't have her dragging the past into J.T.'s life.

He crossed his arms and glanced at the ten-speed bicycle propped against the bay's doorway. "Why don't you just hop on that thing and leave me alone?"

She stood her ground, long gleaming legs locked on the cement floor. "Two things, Mr. Tallchief. One, I want to know why I don't qualify as a customer—there are legal recourses, you know. And two, you are going to accept an invitation to the Tallchiefs. You are going to bring your son to Tallchief house for the dinner they are giving in my honor. That's Friday night. Be there."

"You're telling me what to do, and if I don't cooperate you're going to give that information in your hand to them, right? That's blackmail, isn't it?" Liam inhaled slowly, his usual immense patience stretched by the sensual needs he hadn't expected...and by another woman—Elspeth Tallchief Petrovna. The Tallchiefs had all visited his gas station in the past six months, but one look at Elspeth's quiet gray eyes—what did he sense as their gazes met and locked? Why did the hair on his nape lift as big warning lights blazed in his mind?

"Let's just say I like having my way. You've been avoiding the Tallchiefs, and now you can't. If you're an imposter, they'll know. That's why, isn't it?" Her smirk knocked the breath from him, irritated him and entranced him at the same time.

"Do I or my son look like Tallchief imposters?" He didn't want to enter a conversation with her, but he had and he wasn't backing up. Liam Tallchief had had enough of threats in his life. Without thinking, Liam captured her wrist, and while she was dealing with that, he tugged her toward the sink, rubbed soap compound into her hand and scrubbed it, shaken by the delicate feel of her fingers within his. He dried her hand briskly with a towel and resented cupping her chin in his hand to scrub clean that smudge on her cheek.

Her skin was just as soft as he suspected, contrasting with his darker skin, running smoothly beneath his calluses and scars. He couldn't afford the need to stroke that willful silky hair, to grip it in his fists and hold her still as he took that lush mouth, parted in surprise.

He tossed the towel aside, disgusted with his unstable emotions. "Get out," he said as quietly as he could, not understanding his need to reach out and tug that lean curved body against his. One look down at her T-shirt, which tightened across her breasts as she breathed deeply, caused desire to rake at him.

"Tell me why I don't qualify as a customer. Give me one good reason. I've never been turned down before— for anything. My credit rating is good. I have not written one bad check in my lifetime." She aimed a narrowed, determined look at him. "You handled me like a child. I resent that. And the next time you decide to haul me after you, you're going to end up on your back—on the floor. "

The image of her tossing him, a woman much smaller and lighter than himself, caused a smile to flirt within him. It died when J.T. stirred drowsily on his cot, sitting up to rub his eyes with his small fists.

Liam inhaled roughly. J.T. had heard enough arguments before Reuben passed away. Explaining a sick and dying man's bitterness to a child wasn't easy, because Reuben had been selfish and a bully. Liam had kept Reuben from J.T., because the dying man would be left alone, if he struck out at the boy. "It's all right, J.T. Miss Farrell was just leaving."

"No, I wasn't," she said brightly, and smiled at the little boy. She looked up at Liam, the warmth in her smile dying. "I'd like a date with your son. You're obviously busy, and I'd like to take him for a walk to look at toys and then to the city park playground. Is that okay with you?" she asked, a challenge ringing in her tone. "I'm not running away with him, and you can check out my character with Silver and Nick if you want."

J.T. usually kept his distance from strangers, but the toy offer was too delicious. "Daddy, please?" he asked, tugging on the hammer loop sewn into Liam's carpenter pants.

Michelle was quick to take in the child's familiar grasp on the denim loop. "I wondered," she said. "Men around here usually wear jeans."

"Could be." Liam hefted J.T. up and held him close for a kiss. Still drowsy, J.T. placed his head on Liam's shoulder and cuddled to him. "He doesn't usually take to strangers," he said, holding his son tighter.

J.T. had given him more than he had taken. A child's love and trust reminded Liam of Karen—no qualifications, stipulations or rules—just the simplicity of trust and love.

The woman in front of Liam was a fighter and clearly

used to setting terms. "I'll take very good care of him. We'll only be gone about an hour, and it's time."

It's time. Her statement said he'd kept his son too close, protected him too much and that now it was time for him to— "You've dug in, haven't you?" Liam asked, and disliked sharing his son, though the time would come someday.

As if on cue, J.T. squirmed and pushed away from Liam, who placed him on the floor. J.T. slid his hand into Michelle's free one and stood looking up at his father anxiously. "One hour," Liam heard himself say, his heart tearing slightly. "Back in time for lunch."

"I'll say 'yes' and 'please,' Daddy," J.T. said solemnly, and Liam wished for just a moment that his son was a baby again and he could hold him close and protect him—

Michelle lifted her finger to tip her sunglasses down from the top of her head. They landed neatly on her nose; the gesture was perfected, the silver lenses gleaming up at Liam. She tossed the computer printout of his life onto the work table. "I can always get another copy. See you later, pops," she said with a flashing victorious grin that caused his heart to flip-flop.

"You didn't blackmail me into this," he stated evenly, setting up his defenses.

"No. You're a pushover when it comes to J.T., and he wants to go. But don't try me on the Tallchief matter. I intend to win."

"You're not playing the do-gooder in our lives. Get that straight."

"If I want to do good, Tallchief, I'll do it with this little man." She rubbed J.T.'s glossy hair. "Ready, champ?"

As Liam watched her walk away, the grease mark on

her soft bottom swaying gently, he wondered what had happened. Usually solemn, J.T. was chattering away and showing off his toy truck, and her delighted laughter floated back to Liam. The ache in his heart was for his son, no longer a baby and needing friends. But Liam didn't know how to provide that for J.T., how to blend him with other children, because he'd missed that experience in his own boyhood—

Liam frowned and rubbed the ache in his chest. He didn't understand why he trusted Michelle with his son, or why J.T. was chatting merrily with her now.

He only knew that he wanted her—the raw, sensual pleasure of holding her tight against him. While one message slammed into his body, his mind told him that Michelle Farrell was off-limits.

Two days later Michelle sat cross-legged on Liam's living room floor as J.T. proudly showed her his best toys. She knew Liam couldn't wait to get her out of his rented house, and that was the exact reason she deliberately stayed. With J.T., he'd quickly towed away her car, the sooner to be rid of her—but she wasn't that easily dismissed. Every once in a while she liked to pit herself against an impossible challenge, and Liam qualified as a big one. The repairs would take a week, the dealer had said, and she had all that time to work on getting Liam Tallchief woven into the Tallchief fabric.

Her motive was simple, she told herself: J.T. needed the expansive Tallchief family, to play with children, to enter the activities. Michelle had the background and talent for finding suitable niches, and if Liam wouldn't take action, she would. Liam's lone wolf act, keeping himself away from a family he obviously belonged to, wouldn't help J.T. blend with cousins. If the Tallchiefs were ready to let him do as he wished—well, she wasn't. He would dig into a trench, and as time passed it would deepen, and J.T. would suffer the loss.

His rented house was small, very neat and barren. There were no pictures on the walls other than the bulletin board filled with J.T.'s color crayon drawings. The scarred hardwood floor gleamed, the kitchen no more than a cubbyhole off the small living room. The tiny bathroom she'd used that first night was immaculate, but the fixtures were old, the tub filled with rubber dinosaurs and yellow plastic boats. Proud of his room, J.T. had instantly tugged her into it. A sturdy wooden bed matched a battered dresser, and though not crammed with expensive toys, the room was clearly loved by the little boy. The other bedroom door remained firmly closed, like Liam Tallchief's past.

After two days she'd settled in to nettle him. She recognized, with a soaring, eager sense, that she loved hunting out Liam's dark little edges. He was the best entertainment she'd had in years, and a diversion from the interference of her parents in her life. Liam couldn't say no when J.T. asked if Michelle could come in after their "date" of today. "Don't you have something to do with Nick and Silver?" Liam asked her coolly from the kitchen as he placed the remnants of the meal in the refrigerator.

She savored the dark ridge of temper riding his deep voice. She'd brought take-out dinner to the station— J.T.'s favorite fried chicken, green beans and mashed potatoes—none of them touching on his plate—topped off by chocolate ice cream. "I'm giving my friends some privacy. My vacation is for three weeks, and I can't hoard Silver every minute."

She really enjoyed how Liam stared pointedly at the

clock on the wall. "J.T. should be taking his bath soon and going to bed," he said.

"Good. Then we can talk. I still don't—" Playing the audience for J.T., she clapped as a tiny car shot down a toy ramp and around a plastic curve. He giggled with delight and beamed when she kissed his cheek. Michelle glanced at Liam who had just inhaled sharply, clearly frustrated and displeased. "He's a lovely child. I adore him," she stated quietly. "You can stop wearing those carpenter pants...he's growing up."

Liam's fierce scowl told her to back off, and she wouldn't. An outsider to the beautiful valley, she knew how badly Silver and the rest of the Tallchiefs wanted to become closer to the man who preferred his shadows. She waited while Liam bathed J.T., and when the boy asked, she tucked him in, only to turn to his father's dark expression.

When J.T.'s bedroom door was closed, Liam gripped Michelle's upper arm and turned her to him. She glanced meaningfully at his hand and then up at him. "Don't," she said, aware that his thumb had started to caress her skin.

She feared the sensual interest in his eyes, that dark penetrating look. Liam Tallchief wasn't a man to walk away from, and she wasn't a woman for staying or for playing.

"I don't have time to argue with you," he said, dropping his hand. "You're intruding in our lives. You're not welcome."

"He's growing up, Tallchief. He has a family waiting for him, and they're waiting for you. I've been here only three days, and it's obvious that you can be a real pain in the backside. It's also obvious that the Tallchiefs are too patient, and I'm working on a time line to get this whole gig flowing down the river of success. Now, I could mind my own business—"

"Yes, why don't you?" he invited darkly. "I don't have time for this."

"Make time," she tossed back. "For J.T."

"You think I don't make time for my son?" he asked warningly.

"You're going to the Tallchiefs' on Friday night, and J.T. is going to play with a whole houseful of children with the same black hair and gray eyes. You're going to—"

"Am I? So you're asking me for a date?" he asked carefully, a smile flirting on his gorgeous mouth.

Michelle blinked suddenly, trying to shake the thought from her. Why should she care if his mouth could soften? Why should she want to taste him? "It's not a date exactly. You're just coming. With J.T."

Liam wasn't going to be pushed by her. He wondered how she would react if he pushed back. "You're afraid of something, Ms. Farrell, and you're running. Tell you what—why don't you do the dishes and the laundry, and that will give me thinking time while I'm working on the bills? I usually do housework in the evenings, because I don't have time during the day."

"Me? Do dishes and laundry?" Michelle glanced at the sink of dishes left from breakfast, lunch and J.T.'s snacks. On the table were more dishes, and on the floor in front of the washer and dryer were heaped laundry baskets of clothing.

"Growing boys make lots of laundry. Don't forget to use the stain remover on the chocolate from the ice cream you gave J.T. There's not a housekeeper or a maid in sight. For now, I do it all here, like I make the decisions about our lives."

Clearly Liam was enjoying putting her in a position to leave or to stay and fight. "You should have a house-keeper. You could spend more time with J.T. You could hire a full-time baby-sitter and—"

"So you don't know how to do dishes or laundry, but you're telling me how to manage time with my son. For your information, lady, I tried just that—hiring a full-time housekeeper and baby-sitter. She mistreated my son. I'll never forgive myself for that." With that, Liam cleared the small table of dishes and walked into the kitchen.

"You're willing to give up after one try—" Michelle looked down at the dishcloth Liam had just placed in her hand.

"Sorry. No rubber gloves. No hand cream." He smiled then, one of those gorgeous, I've-got-you grins that caused her heart to race.

"You think I'll leave, don't you? You think I'll back off because of a few dishes and a few conditions. I've met conditions all my life."

"I'll just bet you have."

His tone lacked sincerity, and, challenged, Michelle elbowed him aside. "You're right. I have a housekeeper and a personal assistant who keep things moving smoothly for me."

"Gets the dry cleaning, gets the oil changed in your car, does errands for you? That sort of thing?" he asked too cheerfully, and she knew that he was mocking her.

He wasn't the first to insinuate that her wealth made her life easy. "I've managed. My career is demanding. Most women in my position—"

"Oh, I see."

Another insincere agreement hitched her temper higher. "Look. I'll help with the housework tonight and tomorrow night, if what you're saying is—that you don't have time to socialize. I'll help make time for you, and you'll have no excuse, will you?''

He lifted a black, gleaming eyebrow. ''There's the bathroom to be cleaned. The tub scrubbed, the floor—''

''All right, all right, all right. I get the point. I've butted into your life and you're going to make me pay.''

''No one invited you—'' He reached to the cluttered desk for a stack of envelopes, a checkbook and a pen, and strolled off into the living room. After clicking on a boxing match on the television, he sprawled in a big well-worn chair and smiled innocently back at her.

She could have poured the liquid dish detergent over his head when he said, ''I won't have time to go if I don't get that refrigerator defrosted. Make certain you don't leave any perishables out, will you? And use baking soda in the cleaning water. And I'd like a glass of iced tea when you get a chance.''

Two hours later Michelle plopped down on the couch and glared at Liam. She hurled the dust rag at him. ''Just how are you related to the Tallchiefs?''

Liam folded J.T.'s old diaper, scented of lemon wax and dust. He placed it on his knee and wondered how his son had grown so fast, wearing miniature shorts like his own. He knew little of the Tallchiefs, except that they were orphaned when the eldest—Duncan—was only eighteen, and they'd held the clan together, much to the admiration of Amen Flats. He wasn't certain of the bloodline, except that he descended from the Scots bond-woman and the Native American chieftain who had captured her. There were letters in the wooden chest he'd found after Reuben's death, and he couldn't bear to open them just yet. The postmark had taken him to Amen Flats and for now that was enough.

Two pieces of flint rock, chipped and hard and obviously treasured, lay within a dainty lace handkerchief. They were bound in a length of old red velvet by a leather thong just as old, and still fragrant with an elusive lavender scent. Then, tethered by the thong, was a man's silver ring, dark with age, worn almost thin and circled by Celtic designs. Topped by a simple design of a mountain and a stick man and woman, a small ancient copper box held a bit of dry, frayed straw.

What did they mean? Did he have the right to know?

"...I mean, it's easy to see you're related by the similar coloring and features. But are you cousins or what? Well? Are you just going to sit there brooding? I won't go away until I have answers, you know," Michelle was saying impatiently. "You'd fit in perfectly, if you'd put out one little bit of effort."

"What would you know of fitting in?" he asked too sharply, resenting the anger and frustration this woman could jerk from him. "You think you fit into this small town? You think you fit into my son's life? You think you can push and shove and place people in neat little boxes and everything will be just fine?"

She crossed her arms and glared at him, then tossed her head to dislodge the strand teasing her cheek. "I fit in where I want to. If you weren't so stubborn—"

"You don't fit into a small town, and you know it. Maddy's Hot Spot is the only so-called nightclub in town, and there's not a spa in sight. The women here do their own washing and gardening, and they mind their own business." Liam kept his voice down, resenting the woman tearing into his life. "You're rich, spoiled, probably overeducated, and couldn't manage a simple household budget if you tried."

Michelle leaped to her feet, punched the television button off, and kicked his stocking-covered feet from the footrest. "If I wanted to live here, in Amen Flats, and run my own household, I could."

He didn't bother answering, because the need to stand and kiss her sassy mouth was too strong. "Tell that to someone else, and run back to Daddy, why don't you?"

"I pay my own bills," she said, her voice quivering with emotion. "Where do you get off, anyway?"

"The same place as you. Now get out."

"Friday night. Be there," she said, shooting him a narrow-eyed look before tossing her head.

"Try ordering someone else around," he returned more softly than the emotions racing through him. Then she marched out of his house and slammed the door behind her.

Liam rose to his feet, crossed the room and jerked open the door. Hours later he wished he hadn't seen the moonlight playing in her hair and outlining the sway of her hips and the full curve of her breasts. His instincts told him to capture her, to claim that soft mouth, to fill his hands with her hair and keep her close until she—

The woman was pure trouble—a hot-tempered, pride-filled witch that kept him awake and restless for hours.

Three

For his son, Michelle thought as she watched Liam from Duncan Tallchief's kitchen window. *Liam Tallchief would hole up, alone and wounded from whatever haunted him...but for his son he'd take a step into life.*

His wrecker parked in front of the log and rock home that had been the Tallchiefs' parents'. In the first of August heat, he wore a white dress shirt, turned back at the sleeves, and new Western jeans. He carefully unstrapped J.T. from his car seat and lifted him to the ground. Amid the cars and pickups of the assembled Tallchief clan, Liam held J.T.'s hand and looked up at the ranch house now occupied by Duncan and his family. Behind father and son, the summer sun spread across the lush fields of the ranch, and Liam lifted J.T. on his hip to better survey the ranch that had been inherited by the five Tallchief children.

Within the remodeled ranch house, children played in

front of the rock-hewn fireplace. The home was rich with love and all that was Tallchief, from the tartan draped around Tallchief's spear, to the hand-hewn cradle with a new black-haired baby sleeping in it.

Michelle traced the summer-warm glass at her fingertips. If ever a man belonged to a family, it was Liam to the Tallchiefs. More than legends held the family together—and Liam and J.T. could use that love.

"You did it, and inside of one week. You won't have to do Jasmine's diapers," Silver whispered at her side.

Michelle nodded, her mind instinctively dissecting Liam's personality, trying to slot what she knew of him into neat pigeonholes. The profile didn't fit, odd edges leaping out at her, unanswered questions nudging her need to know everything about him. While Liam would care for J.T., he was definitely a man who preferred the lonely shadows. Michelle shrugged mentally and, allowing for the kitchen's heat, tossed the thick braid created by one of the beautiful children from her shoulder.

Whatever ran through Liam Tallchief, it wasn't ice. When he'd held her, when he shot her one of those dark, sizzling looks, the jolt had burned through to her bones. She could still feel his muscles tense, as if he meant to keep her—as if nothing could tear her from him. She frowned, trying to place her emotions in neat order, and failed.

Duncan's wife, Sybil, came to stand beside Michelle. "You've done a lovely thing, Michelle. Liam has been polite and cool, keeping to himself. We know he's here for a reason and we don't care. Elspeth was troubled from the first moment she saw him, and that's enough. Some call her intuitive, but she's more than that. Una had seer blood, and from Tallchief Elspeth gained her shaman strength. She's an herbalist and a weaver, weaving more into her products than wool—there is heart and love and strength—and she feels something deep for Liam.''

"I'm an outsider, but even I know this is right," Michelle said softly. "That little boy is a mirror image of the other children, and Liam is, too—oh, look. The men have gone out to praise that beast of a machine. Look at that. Look at Liam and J.T. amid Duncan, Birk, and Calum. He's the same—that black hair, slashing brows, those cutting cheekbones and rock-solid jaws—"

"He loves that little boy. Poor thing, he doesn't know what to do with all those tall men who look like his father. Look at him cling to Liam," Sybil noted.

"Aye, he does look like us." Elspeth came to quietly stand at the window, her hair as glossy as her brothers'. Her gray eyes were dark with emotions, her expression still as if she waited—

At her sister's side, Fiona laughed and juggled a sleepy baby on her hip. "Your Alek looks like a gypsy amid our brothers, and my Joel and his brothers, Nick and Rafe, look exactly alike. They're gorgeous, aren't they? Hunks, every one. They're having too much fun out there alone. Let's send the children down on them."

When the other women moved away, Elspeth stood next to Michelle, and her silence as she studied Liam said more than words. "He's come home," she said quietly, drawing the Tallchief tartan around her, despite the summer heat. "He'll find pain and he'll find joy—"

Then Elspeth turned, the shadows lifting as she studied Michelle. "You're a soldier, aren't you? Doing what is expected and yet you're wanting more. You've taken on a crusade because of your love of Silver, and in giving, you'll find more than you could have ever believed possible for you as a woman."

"What do you mean?" Michelle whispered, aware and

shaken by the strength of Elspeth's statement. She smoothed the pearl studs in her lobes, chosen to reflect a polished professional image in a harsh business world.

"Time," Elspeth returned. "With Liam, everything will take time to unravel. But you have your own journey, too, as a woman. You can't always arrange life to suit you. It doesn't place happiness in neat little niches. You like a good fight, a challenge to sharpen your teeth, and Liam has stirred your need to conquer. You'll have a hard time of that with him. He's like my brothers—savages one minute and scared in their boots the next, if a woman cries."

While Michelle struggled with that, Elspeth turned to the window again. "Look there, amid the children—J.T. just starting to smile...."

Michelle smoothed her hair, and the tight waves bumped gently beneath her fingertips. *Sunlit witch's silk,* Liam had said, stirring that wild restlessness inside her. She had a temper, of course, but her mind ruled it—until Liam Tallchief. When he'd held her in the storm, she'd loved the wind in her hair, the rain on her skin and her lashes, her mouth. She shook her head, and her braid rippled down her back. She always did what was expected—except for leaving her father's company and divorcing the son-in-law he'd handpicked. She kept very close to the rules and something about Liam Tallchief made her want to break them.

"I should have minded my own business," she murmured, and wondered if she could manage a timely headache. Liam Tallchief was just too much. "You know he made me clean his house. He actually bargained with me, when he probably knew he was coming all the time. He's contrary, illogical, and when I think of all the laundry, the bathroom and the floor scrubbing—'Bring me a glass of iced tea,' he said. It was there in his eyes, taunting me, saying that I'd never lifted a broom or kept a house and that he wanted to play lord to my servant role, just to set me off.''

"Aye, he's like the rest, a despicable pig,'' Elspeth murmured, humor curling her lips. "And a challenge, just the same.''

"I've had enough challenges in my life, just to survive, and I'm not needing another one.'' Michelle skipped the background check that she'd used to threaten him. Anyone with enough skills could have pulled the information out of the computers easily enough…and Liam knew it. There were many legal reasons why his name might not have been Tallchief, though he evidently was related. Why had he changed his name and his son's? Why did he wipe the name Cartwright from him as though it were so much mud?

"You helped him. It's not in you to sit on the sidelines when you see someone you love troubled, and Silver sees him like the outsider she was. She's tried desperately to get him to come to their home. But he's a hunter, like Tallchief, and my father was the best tracker in the country. Now my brothers are, and they like to hunt, treasuring the chase. I've an idea that Liam questions anything that comes too easily to him, like the invitations of our families. He's very cautious and sets his own terms.''

"He should be more appreciative. You're a caring family. You've all given Silver so much when no one else could help. When her twin died at sixteen, she almost did, too. I loved them both and I was so helpless. I just wanted to help all of you. This family is exceptional, and J.T. should be a part of it. Not every family could forgive the sons of the man who murdered their parents. Yet all three of the murderer's sons, the Palladins, married Tallchiefs. J.T. should know of the traditions of Una and Tallchief.''

Elspeth was silent, but smiled softly. She drew a tiny waving tendril from Michelle's cheek, studying it in the filtered sunlight of the window. ''The boy has snagged your heart and you're fighting for him and maybe for yourself, too. Tallchief made many cribs, you know, to earn money for his family. Sybil, Duncan's wife, is a genealogist and loves a good hunt for treasures. She brought the original one to Duncan, the one Tallchief gave to Una for their five babies. Una wouldn't marry him without a dowry, so he made the first and gave it to his father to keep her pride. My mother worked on Una's journals, and I helped. Sybil sometimes finds items related to our family. She's always trying to find another crib. She's working on that now.''

''Another Tallchief baby?''

''Maybe,'' Elspeth said lightly and smiled lightly as she turned away.

At the dinner table later, J.T. sat on Liam's lap and shyly smiled at Emily, Sybil's college-age daughter. Emily tossed her red hair, and Joel Palladin's preteen son, Cody, let out a love-struck, worshipful sigh. A known charmer and confident of her powers, she smiled at him and riffled J.T.'s hair. ''Hey, little man. Why don't you come sit on my lap and let your daddy eat his homemade ice cream?''

J.T.'s tentative smile said he wanted to, but— He looked up at Liam, who nodded solemnly. Liam had been too quiet, his smoky gaze slowly taking in the big family room. He tensed when he noted the barn board stamped with the Tallchief Cattle Ranch stick man and mountain, and his big hand crushed the woven napkin, the knuckles white. *Why had he frowned so fiercely?*

He breathed hard, the vein in his throat throbbing beneath his dark skin. As though sensing Michelle's study, his face jerked to hers, and she saw his pain, mixed with anger. He resented her seeing that—inside him where the dark mysteries flowed, into the man he was, kept from others. To let him know that she'd seen and would not be turned away, Michelle smiled sweetly and fluttered her lashes. She hadn't much experience in touting feminine airs, but the moment was too good to pass.

Liam tore his fierce scowl from his face and met her smile, the warmth not rising to his eyes. Then he looked to the red Native American shield that had been Tallchief's, and the old cradle rich with Celtic images and scarred by teething babies. Elspeth's rugs and woven goods circled the home, and more than once, Duncan—known as The Defender—searched out Liam's gaze. The message was from male to male, locking and holding and sliding away to pin Michelle. Unfamiliar with the dark intense look, Michelle shivered when Liam's gaze brushed her mouth.

Fire and storms lashed at her again, drying her mouth and sending her heart fluttering in her throat. She knew she'd long remember the uncivilized hard taste of his mouth, a burning stamp across her own. She hated the trembling of her fingers locked to her iced water glass, an obvious note that he was getting to her. In another instant, if Liam did not stop that smoky, intent stare, she'd dump the—

From then on, J.T. moved into the mass of Tallchief children, his hand locked tightly in Emily's. "You look enough alike to be one of my uncles and I'm going to claim you as another of my Black Knights. Duncan rescued me when I was a child, but I claim all the Tallchief men as my knights. They've been there often enough for me. You can call me princess like they do, and I baby-sit, you know,'' she said, grinning at Liam. ''Can he ride horses? I'd take good care of him.''

J.T.'s eyes widened. ''Horses? Me? Ride?''

Clearly the little boy worshipped Emily. One look at Liam told Michelle that he was already regretting the boy's growing up. Then Birk bent to playfully nuzzle his heavily pregnant petite wife, and she elbowed him with enough strength to make him grunt. Retaliating, Birk brought Lacey's small hand to his mouth to kiss her palm. The humble gesture was so sincere and filled with love that Michelle almost found herself sighing.

But then, she was a practical woman and she'd completed her mission, breaking a fingernail earlier as she had stacked his dishes in the cupboard. Liam Tallchief deserved no more of her time, though she hoped to see J.T. whenever she could.

''Da-da?'' Ian Palladin, Fiona's toddler son chirped and patted Liam's arm.

''Case of mistaken identity,'' Talia, Calum's wife, said with a grin. ''Poor baby is confused. Joel, Rafe and Nick Palladin all look alike, and so do the Tallchief boys, but Alek is a loner—''

'''Boys'?'' Calum, known as Calum the Cool, purred with a slow, hot look at his wife.

''Liam does look like one of the brothers,'' Sybil murmured, tracing his features and then turning to study the matching ones of her husband, Duncan.

As the rest of the family talked and ate and teased each other, Michelle studied Liam, looking after his son, his expression sad. On a sudden impulse, she didn't know why—because she wasn't a woman who showed affection easily—Michelle patted his cheek.

His aching pain was quickly slashed away by searing anger. "Leave me alone," he said too quietly.

"You made a choice and it was for your son. J.T. needs this and so do you, whether you're liking it now or not.... Stand and fight," she whispered back, shaking with her own anger. She jabbed a finger into his chest and didn't remove it when he looked slowly, meaningfully down. She prodded him again, careless of the hard, tense muscles running beneath the cloth. "You took the name Tallchief, didn't you? 'Stand and fight' is one of their phrases, used in hard times."

"I choose what I take," he returned curtly with a touch of arrogance much like Tallchief must have used.

"Then take this," she murmured more coolly than she felt as she stood away from the table. She lifted her glass of ice water to pour over his head. While Liam glared at her and ice water dripped down his face, Michelle raised her head proudly. She wouldn't apologize—not to him. Horrified, she stared at the water dripping to the place mat woven with Celtic and Native American images. She'd totally embarrassed herself and the expensive charm school that her father had forced her to attend. Her cheeks were hot, her dignity was on the hand-braided rug at her feet, and down the long table, the adult Tallchief family studied her. While smiles flirted around their mouths, their eyes held a knowing look.

J.T. giggled suddenly, clapped his hands, and Liam's head jerked to his son. The boy began to laugh outright, the sound delightful. When Liam turned back to look up at Michelle, she didn't trust his dark, dangerous look...nor her own wild mood. With as much dignity as she could scrape up from the rug, she managed, "I think I'll just take a walk. Excuse me, please."

In the next moment she was hurrying down the path

to Tallchief Lake, careless of the brush tugging at her head and body. She lived her life in logical one-two-three steps, acted logically, and now she'd just dumped a glass of ice water over a man's head—in front of a family she adored. She began to run, careless of the cream silk designer blouse and loose black silk slacks. The strap of one Italian-made sandal tore away, caught on a bush, and she hobbled along the rest of the distance to the shore of the dark, brooding lake. A gentle wind stirred the reeds along the river bank and rippled the water.

Tallchief Mountain, etched with fir and pines, dappled with tiny meadows and jutting rocks, soared up into the sunset, shading the lake. Michelle hobbled to a rock, careful of the torn strap, and sank down upon it, ready to brood.

The chirps of frogs and birds and the sweet scent of lush grass wove around her as she sat, chin braced upon her raised knees, her arms circling her legs. She turned to the sound of a twig snapping, fearing a bear or a wolf prowling in the shadows before night. The outline of Liam Tallchief's tall body was unmistakable, but just as predatory. Shivering again with anger, she turned back to study the dark, mystical lake, the waves gently patting the shore. "You're too much trouble, even for a bet," she said, meaning it. A second thought had her turning around again, searching the shadows. "You didn't bring J.T. out here, did you?"

"No. I don't want him to see the fight we're about to have, and for once, playing with the Tallchief children, he didn't care where I was. He knows I'll be back. I'm always there when he needs me, but he's too excited with his new friends—what's this about a bet?"

"I bet Silver that I'd get you here, and I did. That's all there is to it." She didn't want him to know that her

efforts were on her own behalf, too, not just to avoid
Jasmine's diapers. She wanted to see him again, amid the
family that he obviously belonged within—

"All those dishes and scrubbing for a bet?" he pushed.

"J.T. was worth it. They're his cousins. They're a
match for coloring and features, and so are you," she
added, and waved her hand airily. "Fight away. It takes
two, and I'm done talking with you."

"My relationship with the Tallchiefs is my business.
And the next time you get bored and want to play, pick
on someone else." He snagged her wrist and tugged her
to her feet. When she swung her free hand at him, he
caught it, holding her immobile. "You're going to go
back there and apologize to that family for disrupting
their dinner."

While she was working up a good scalding brew of
what she thought of him, Liam placed both her wrists in
one hand and tugged the band binding her braid, tossing
it away. Then his fingers were in her hair, working it free
of the weave. When she struggled against him, her hair
flew out into the slight evening breeze and whirled
around her head. He sank his fingers into the freed
strands, capturing her as he studied her furious expression. "You always get your way, don't you? You're used
to plowing right over people to get what you want."

She tried to toss her head and failed, her hair captured
by his fist. "I got you here, didn't I?"

"I would have come, anyway. Eventually. I like
choosing the time and place. I just liked watching those
expensively tended hands, decked out in those flashing
diamonds, doing J.T.'s and my laundry."

"You would not have— You haven't visited with
them in six months. Perverse, arrogant— You're enjoying this, aren't you? Trapping a poor defenseless woman,

out here— Don't deny it. I see it in your eyes, in that grin. You're enjoying taunting me—Why?''

"Someone has to. Everyone else just lets you run over them and you're not defenseless. You've got a cutting tongue, lady.'' In the evening shadows, with the moon beginning to peek over Tallchief Mountain, Liam's devastating grin widened.

She stood still and tossed her head, looking away from him. When he tossed that reckless, boyish grin at her, he was too dangerous. She didn't trust the pitter-pat of her racing heart for one moment. "You'll get bored, holding me captive. That's illegal, you know. You'll—''

"Will I? You want to bet on that, too?'' His gray eyes flowed over her hair, a thumb reaching to stroke a strand waving across her hot cheek. Desire poured from him, weaving around her, and, inexperienced with sensual play, Michelle shivered. "You want to slot me into a pigeonhole, to understand something that doesn't concern you? At the Tallchiefs, Silver said you are divorced. Let's talk about your ex-husband. He let you walk all over him, didn't he? And then you walked out.''

It was the truth. Oliver hadn't resisted anything she wanted, even the divorce. It was her father who fought— "Let's talk about your wife, shall we?'' she cut back at Liam.

She hadn't expect the tender shadows enveloping him as he spoke. "Sweet, sensitive, loving. I loved her. She died when J.T. was born, and I'll never forgive myself for letting her talk me into the pregnancy. She wasn't well—''

"You regret your son? That beautiful, sweet baby?'' Michelle's statement cut harshly into the night.

"No. He's everything to me. Karen gave him to me, and he was what she wanted, to leave a bit of herself alive and healthy as she'd never been…. This is what I do regret—'' Then his hand cupped the back of her head, and he took her mouth, searing her with heat, fusing his lips to hers. The stormy emotions locked her immobile and she could do nothing, but taste and feel. She slanted her head to tighten the fight, and the pleased, hungry growl coming from low in Liam's throat was a unique, first pleasure. He freed her wrists and filled his fists with her hair, his mouth moving eagerly, hungrily upon hers. His scent filled her, the heat of his body, and she was soaring to a heavenly, exciting place she'd never been—

She had to capture him, to hold him close, and she touched his hard stomach, smoothed the ridges with her fingertips and heard his sharp inhaling breath against her cheek. He stood still, shivering, heat pouring from him, his hands trembling as they left her hair and began stroking her back. He was giving her a choice, she sensed, to take or to walk away—

Then those stormy gray eyes moved slowly down her body to the shirt torn by the brush on her run to the lake and freed of its upper buttons. His gaze locked on her breasts, clad in beige lace and with a big hand open upon her back, he gently eased her against him, watching the fit of their bodies. He breathed shallowly, his features harsh, and she knew that one word, one movement would free her.

She desperately wanted him to touch her, to cup the soft flesh he was studying, nestled against his chest, that dark passionate expression branding her. She held him tight, anchoring him close. This powerful, beautiful man wanted, and yet would not take without permission— She didn't know how to tempt him, and when she breathed deeply, her flesh rising against his, he groaned unsteadily. Slowly, watching her, he lifted his hand to carefully, rev-

erently mold her breast. His thumb ran across the crest
of a hardened nipple and he circled it slowly. She could
no more have moved than she could start her heart beating again—the magical touch sucked away her breath and
made her head spin.

"Why haven't you had children, pretty witch? The real
reason, not the canned words you've prepared for others," he asked roughly, caressing her as her hands slid
upward in the storm of unsteady emotions, to dig into his
hard, safe shoulders.

"I haven't felt the need—" The rest of the words were
caught by his lips, the kiss gentle now, searching and
tempting and heating. His hands locked around her waist,
then eased to her hips, fingers digging in slightly. She
knew then, deep within her, that she'd needed a man to
hold her tight, to test her strength as a woman. She
needed a force equal to hers, to the wild, reckless calling
within her—kept hidden too long. She parted her lips
against the gentle nudge of his tongue and quivered as
the kiss deepened, heat rocking their bodies, much as the
earth trembled around a volcano before it released the
red-hot lava—

Liam's hands caressed a downward path to smooth her
bottom and then eased her closer to his hardened desire.
His whisper was hoarse and unsteady against her lips,
"Don't play games. I don't. The air is filled with your
body's sweet warmth mixed with that wildflower—"

The statement was shocking, elemental, but she refused to acknowledge the damp warmth of her body, her
arousal amid the other scents. The wildness leaped within
her, hot and barely controlled and aching to be free—
when had she ever been truly free? To take and give
and— She'd always been controlled, but now she wanted

to tear away Liam's white dress shirt and press herself against him.

"You're aroused," she whispered back, though they were alone in the cool August night beside the lake. The novelty of seducing a man as quickly and as thoroughly as she had Liam went straight to that empty, aching hole in her life, filling her with a warm, fuzzy womanly emotion she didn't dare define.

"Could be," he whispered, easing to nibble on her ear. "Probably not. It's a condition that comes upon me infrequently, every few years or so. But you're not my type, so I'm probably not aroused. If I were, and admitted it, you'd probably run back to your nice safe little office."

"I don't run. I have a huge office and I could seduce you right here on this rock and you know it," she stated, the warm, fuzzy womanly emotion fading away, replaced by a nettling anger.

"Nope. I'm not in the mood," he said quite cheerfully, and freed her, stepping back on the rock.

He grabbed her wrists, just as she pushed him hard, tumbling them both into the cold, black lake. When she surfaced, sputtering and angry, Liam was grinning at her in the moonlight. She splashed water at him, muttered about the ways she would murder him and began to work her way up the marshy bank. She slid, her shoe with the broken strap floating away into the lake with her not-so-dependable control. Liam snatched the sandal, stuffed it in his pocket and chuckled. When she turned to glare at him, he splashed her.

Michelle decided to retreat from the playful, boyish devastation grinning up at her. She turned and gripped the reeds, which came free, and she hurled them back at him. "Can't take it, can you?" he asked, chuckling.

"I choose what I take," she returned hotly, reminding him of his arrogant statement.

"Is that right?" Coming up behind her, Liam supported her with both big hands, helping as she crawled the rest of the way up the bank. The undignified retreat nicked at her pride, and she wanted to fly at Liam, careless of the consequences.

One look down her torn silk blouse and slacks and Michelle rounded on Liam, quivering with anger. They stood on the flat rock now, his hands on his hips as he watched her struggle for words. "You're muddy," he said, watching her, waiting for her to ignite.

"I'm wet," she finally managed. "I'm wet and muddy and not very happy at the moment."

He tilted his head, eyeing her curiously as water dripped from his shaggy hair. "Is that the best you can do?"

"This is a French designer outfit, and now it's ruined. Give me my shoe," she said, snatching her sandal from his chest pocket.

While she glared accusingly up at him, Liam's gaze slowly warmed a path down to her muddied blouse. The silk lay intimately upon her, outlining her breasts. In the moonlight her nipples peaked against the damp cloth.

Liam slowly began to unbutton his shirt, and Michelle's heart began to race. She wanted to run—she wanted to hurl herself against him, fist his hair as he had hers and take…. Uneasy with her emotions and wanting to distract him, she began to talk. "The Tallchief bridal tepees are placed beside the lake—"

"Take off your blouse."

"What? You can't possibly—"

"What? Have you? Here?" He grinned down at her and waggled her head as if she were a child. "I'll turn

my back," he explained too patiently, watching her reaction. "You can wear my shirt back—yours reveals
more than it hides now."

"There's no need to turn your back. We're both
adults," she said, struggling to be worldly. He wasn't
forcing her to act prudish; she wasn't. Her fingers trembled over the buttons as she met his look, daring him to
taunt her further. Liam's eyes darkened as he unbuttoned
his shirt and held it loosely at his side. "Here. Hold
this," she said, handing her blouse to him.

He tucked a length of her shirt into his back pocket
and, still holding her eyes, began to carefully ease her
into his shirt. He buttoned it slowly, carefully, as if placing his thoughts in order with each button. "This cheap
cotton is a bit more concealing that your silk and lace....
You're a hothead, Ms. Farrell. A volatile woman—"

"Am not." She resented the childish statement fling-
ing from her lips. After all she was a businesswoman, an
executive—

"Hot-blooded and sweet and bewitching," he added,
lifting her hair away from the shirt's collar to study the
strands clinging to his fingers in the moonlight. "But a
little too much trouble."

With that, he bent slightly and hefted her over his
shoulder. While Michelle held her sandal and wondered
what had happened, Liam began to walk back to the Tallchiefs. "You'd better put me down," she yelled, and
began squirming.

The big hand on her bottom kept her still and locked
to him. Unused to being handled, Michelle tried her best
to be poised—but then dangling over a man's broad
shoulder didn't allow much for dignity. He did put her
down in front of the assembled Tallchief family, and

when she whipped around to tell him exactly where to go, he grinned. "You said 'put me down.'"

As if it were evidence before the jury, he reached to his back pocket and handed the muddy blouse to her. To the Tallchiefs standing on the big front porch, he said, "She can't talk right now. She's in a snit and she apologizes."

Then he placed his big hand on her head and waggled it gently, playfully, until she slashed it away. Michelle looked up at his smile and the humor lighting his gray eyes and wanted to toss him onto the ground and thoroughly mash him, kiss that smile from his lips and explore that lovely, gleaming broad chest. But pride and temper ruled her, and she managed to grasp a small measure of control as she marched up the steps, carrying her shoe. "It was a lovely dinner and a lovely swim, and Mr. Tallchief assures me that he'll be coming back to visit you. But I'm going home now, to Silver's. Business calls, you know," she lied with as much dignity as she could summon. "Thank you for the wonderful evening."

Four

The next afternoon Elspeth opened the door at the first knock. In her mind, while tending her herbs, she'd seen Liam Tallchief walking toward her, his heart questioning. Wanting to have Liam to herself, she'd asked Alek to take the children to the ice cream parlor. Loving a woman descended from a Scottish seer and a Native American shaman, Alek knew when her senses were prowling. She looked up at the man filling her doorway, his face masked in the shadows of the past. He looked so much like her brothers, but while their pain had been eased by love, Liam wore his scars like a silent cloak. "I'm glad you came," she said simply. "Time for fresh applesauce cake and iced tea, and time to talk," she added, sensing his need and noting the small wooden chest tucked beneath his arm.

Liam wore a clean, long-sleeved cotton shirt and the loose carpenter pants she'd seen his son gripping tightly.

She ached for him, a man alone and trying his best for his son. "Emily is baby-sitting, then. She's got a way with children, especially the boys. She'll be off again to college soon, and leaving a trail of broken hearts," she said as she led Liam into her workroom, filled with Una's loom and the herbs that would dye the Tallchief wool into colored yarn.

For what she must do, Elspeth chose the most familiar setting, the room layered with her weaving and her family's past. Una's journals stacked neatly on one shelf, waiting for Liam. Scents from the hanging lavender bundles curled around her, and she prayed that this lonely, scarred man would find peace. He looked surprised at the small table she'd prepared, applesauce cake cut on plates and served with iced tea on her woven place mats. She'd known he would come, when that quiet, troubled gaze sought hers at the Tallchiefs'. Michelle Farrell had him brooding, a strong woman tossed into the tempest of his life. Liam Tallchief had much to settle, and Elspeth would try. "Sit. Let's talk," she invited, aching for him as he noted the huge loom Tallchief had fashioned for Una, a weaver. "I learned from my mother and she from hers, and then some from Una's journals. She was a woman alone, except for her love, in a strange, frightening country, and I think the journals helped. He loved her of course, though she wounded his pride."

"You knew I was coming. I've heard you can—"

Elspeth shrugged, making light of the senses that prowled within her, telling her the future and of the past. Liam was silent, sipping his tea, the small chest at his feet. He met her eyes finally, after taking his fill of the room, cluttered with yarn and a spinning wheel and the massive loom. "It's too much," he said quietly.

"I know. The feelings are in you as they are in us, but we've had time to understand. It's new to you."

As tall and powerful as her beloved Alek, Liam ran a rough hand down his jaw. "I want this for my son," he said unevenly. "I'm leaving the chest—for now. It was found with me. There are letters inside from your mother and other things. I'd like those things back, please. When you're finished."

"The letters seemed too private, a woman writing to another woman?" A woman who had raised and fought with her brothers, Elspeth knew that honor ran deep within Liam. "Who told you?"

He breathed deeply, sucking in the past and releasing into her keeping a scarred wound reopened, and pain ran through the shadows of his face. "Mary Cartwright. Wife of Reuben, who carried me home from my parents' wrecked car and gave me to her—to raise as a son. You're right, I don't like women's letters and for a reason. I found a letter from Mary after Reuben died—she'd hidden it. Mary was already gone, so was my wife—Karen died giving birth to J.T. I want more for my son than I had," he said more strongly, emotion threading his deep voice. "*I had a son and didn't even know who I was.* What I was."

"None of it was your fault. You'll find what you need. Give it time. You know you're named for Liam Tallchief, one of the five children of Una and Tallchief." And so Elspeth told Liam of how Elizabeth Montclair, an English noblewoman, and her hunting party had been trapped by the lawless on Tallchief Mountain. Forced by the outlaws to save her sister and herself, Elizabeth entered the tent and took the fierce, fighting man staked to the ground within her. It pleased the renegade band that an English lady would mount an unwilling man, a half-blood staked to the ground, and let him pierce her virgin body. Furious that he had no choice and that she had taken his seed from him, Liam had hated her. Then she was safe back in England, away from the raw land. But the child she bore was his, and he claimed them both, pirating them back to Tallchief land. "She came to love him, and they treasured each other. But the taming wasn't easy for both of them. She threw away her jewels to save his pride, and he gave her his heart."

"I want J.T. to know love. How it feels," Liam stated, emotion rumbling in his tone.

"You love him. He knows that."

She could have cried when Liam lifted his pain-filled eyes to hers and said, "I'm not certain I know about love. How to give it."

"Then it's time," she whispered, her heart bleeding for him.

"I have to be ready...inside. I can't just read them."

"You will be." She hugged her mother's letters tight against her, and fought damning the murderer who took her parents away too soon. "I'll keep them for you, and we'll talk again. Thank you. I loved my mother very much."

"You'll see to my son, if I'm late tonight? You'll take care of him?" he asked, the desperation in his voice slicing through her.

"Aye, I will. Rest easy on that, Liam Tallchief, and do what you must," she answered. The man had been too alone, fearing for his son's safety over his own. "We'll tend him well, if anything ever happened to you. He's one of us, and so are you. When you claimed the name Tallchief as your right, we claimed you."

"It's the feeling," he whispered. "That I am a part of a family. That I am not. That I have a heritage I don't understand. Not just the bloodline, but what goes with it. Storms move inside me and other needs I haven't explored. You know, don't you, that Reuben Cartwright made me what I am?''

Other needs, Elspeth repeated silently. Michelle had raised those fierce needs to take and to claim, and, being a controlled man, walking in shadows, Liam wasn't prepared for the urgent calling.

''Your past was cold and hard. You aren't. You did what you had to do to survive, to provide for your son. When it's time, we'll have tea again, and I'm glad you're not as ill-mannered as my brothers. Birk calls my teatime 'torture and drinking grass.' Thank goodness I don't have to tend them anymore.... I want you to have this—''

She rose from the table and took a folded length of tartan sash from the shelf. ''It's the Tallchief plaid, blue and 'dragon-green' and vermillion for Tallchief. And I'll have no complaining as my brothers did, when I finish your kilt. No crude comments about the cold wind blowing up your backside. You'll be wearing it like the rest and tearing the heart from the ladies, just as they do, the beasts. J.T. will have one, too.''

On top of the folded tartan, Elspeth placed a small neat journal. ''It's Elizabeth Montclair Tallchief's. You'll find out more about our heritage, and you won't be faced with your past just yet. Sometimes these things are better to ease into…when you are ready. I'll do what I can to help you with that journey. You take your time, Liam Tallchief. I'll see that J.T. is cared for.''

''A few hours on the mountain. By myself, then I'll be back,'' he said, holding the tartan very carefully as if he'd never been given gifts before. She nodded and promised herself that Liam would see more gifts—and love—coming his way. Softness and love and gifts hadn't been in Liam's life, and his big hands trembled, his expression humbled.

After Liam had gone, Elspeth called Duncan. "Duncan the Defender, you are not to tuck Michelle Farrell under your wing. A battle is brewing between her and Liam and you are not to interfere."

She listened to him rumble a protest, and smiled. Elspeth hung up the telephone and set her mind to the task of studying the letters from her mother to Tina Tallchief, Liam's rightful mother. When the wreck occurred, Liam's parents were coming to visit the Tallchiefs, to discover their heritage, just as their son would do now. Elspeth opened Una's journals and held the letters close, trying to see into the past. "It's the flint and the fire," she said finally, too drained to move. "Liam's time has come, and he'll find more pain before he finds peace. He's not a man who can burst into a new world, and each step will take him closer to more of what he has lost—a family torn apart by a selfish man. Liam is methodical, taking in one piece of the puzzle at a time. He was so humble accepting the Tallchief plaid, I could have cried."

She ran her fingertips across the small tooled copper box—the mountain symbol and the stick man and woman—and the flints. "Aye, flint and fire."

Liam made his way up Tallchief Mountain, across the tiny lush meadows filled with August sunflowers, the jutting rocks high above him. The path was worn, but he felt it call to him, driving him upward. A chipmunk chattered, running up the red bark of a pine, the scents of earth and woods circling Liam, coming inside him. Whatever rode him now was instinctive, and he shivered, tearing a wild rose from the briar, ignoring the slight burn of the thorns. He sucked the clean air into him, felt it surge through his body, then tore away the shirt he'd worn for the lady called Elspeth.

The plaid unfurled in the breeze and he swung it under one arm and over the other shoulder. He pressed the woven length over his pounding heart, woven by a woman whose senses and heart told her more than her eyes— Elspeth Tallchief Petrovna had claimed him as one of her own, a brother to tend and love. She terrified him—a man of shadows. "Aye," he whispered softly, testing the Tallchief word upon his lips. He knew that at last his son was safe, and should something happen to him, Elspeth would love J.T. as her own.

That terror lifted, he opened himself to feeling.

Who was he? Why did the Rocky Mountain sky seem bluer, more free than before? Why did his blood pound, his senses come alive?

He tore his shirt, pushing away the echoes of Reuben's harsh, stingy training. Liam made a sash for the sweat upon his forehead, then scanned the highland meadows that must have called to Una, the Scots bondwoman captured by Tallchief. *Free,* Liam thought. *I'm free. This is what I am.* He listened to his heart, his senses alive, in tune with the mountain. A slight noise took his stare to the deer grazing in the meadow decked with daisies and sunflowers. A scent took him crouching beside a fragrant plant. In the tumbling stream, the rocks were round and dull in reds and blues, and fish waited to be caught. The sun stroked his body, the slight breeze curling around him, enveloping him. Lavender scents clung to the plaid draped around his body, and he smiled at the thought of his legs in a kilt. "Not a chance."

But he was a father, too, and Liam's head jerked toward Amen Flats and to the rented house where J.T.

would be napping under Emily's care. *His son needed this—the scents and colors and the wonderful sense of freedom.*

He walked slowly around the meadow, startling the deer, brushing his palm against the thick grass and taking into him what he had lost. Then, settling upon a rock, he opened Elizabeth Tallchief's small journal, and let himself step into the past. "That fine beast of a man came after me and his son. He crossed the ocean, and he dressed like a gentlemen at court, but I knew what he was—a savage, set upon me and claiming his son. I could have killed him, and I dearly tried. Hard as flint he was, and angry, too, for me taking his seed as he lay staked upon the ground, and making our beautiful boy.... But one look at those fierce, stormy eyes and I caught fire, testing myself against him—"

Liam smoothed his big hand over the woman's beautiful cursive writing, uncertain of the emotions riding him. Uncomfortable with reading Elizabeth's story, for he had found too much in another woman's letters, Liam forced himself to read on—to understand for his son's sake. "When a man and a woman, equally matched, strike against each other, fire will fly—just as two flints strike sparks off each other. 'Tis a game, finding the strength of a man and challenging that truth. I am a woman used to having my way, and being captured by a man who had fathered my child was no easy matter. How I battled with him—that great hard man, Liam Tallchief, scarred by life. He did not yield to me, nor would I have him be less than he was. But in the end, he filled my heart, and a softness grew between us. I knew no other would make me feel so alive. No other could take my heart as Liam Tallchief. When he held our son and that gentleness came upon him, I knew—I claimed him with a ring and marked him for my own. For his part, he gave me two flints, the tinderbox marked with the Tallchief symbol, and a love that burns true.''

Liam carefully placed the journal inside the folded tartan, treasuring both. The tinderbox design in his wooden chest matched that of the Tallchief brand, a mountain with a stick man and a woman. The cradle that Tallchief had made Una to replace the one she'd brought from Scotland, had those same designs. Liam, his namesake, had fought through guards, kidnapped the woman who had kept his son secret. He kept Elizabeth stewing on the voyage back to Tallchief land and—

Liam rubbed his hands over his face— He'd lost so much, his son had lost so much.... ''Gentleness came upon him'' was exactly how he felt when holding J.T. As if all the world settled into peace, wrapped in a child's love.

The woman who had leaped into his mind and hardened his body was another matter. Michelle ripped peace from him and tore it apart with those slender, elegant fingers. He wanted to bury himself in her, taking her mouth—but those dreams were dangerous for a man who found more comfort in silence and being alone. Michelle wasn't for him—and he didn't believe in love, other than his son's. All that he asked of life was to safely raise his son—more than that seemed too much.

His fist clenched upon his knee. What would he know of treating a woman as she deserved? What would he know of the soft sweet night talk that women were supposed to love? What did he have to offer a woman—the icy hard ways he'd learned too early?

He'd tried hard to change with Karen, but he'd been paying bills for Reuben's garage and medical expenses. He'd been too harsh with his wife, when she'd wanted a few dollars for kitchen curtains—Liam squeezed his eyes shut and hated the words that came so freely to his mouth—"I'm trying to make a living, dammit. There's no money for silliness...."

He scrubbed his rough hands across his face. He'd regretted the words instantly, and Karen had loved him just the same. But he had steel for a heart, and it was better he kept to himself where women were concerned....

Then a sound took his narrowed eyes to the trail and across the lush meadow, to the beautiful witch with her fascinating green eyes shot from the forest's shadows. Her long, waving hair caught the sun and the wind, and Liam's gaze took in her body, the breeze pushing her clothing tight against her. His instincts told him to take her, to fuse his mouth to hers, to hold her and to grasp the fire that only she could give him.

Michelle glanced at the lengthening shadows and kicked the rock in the worn path. "He's up here somewhere, and I want to tell him exactly what I think of him."

A noise in the thicket turned her, and Liam's broad chest gleamed in the half-light. She looked the long distance up into his steely eyes, that hard face. "You need a haircut," she said, forcing herself to slash at him, when she wanted to fist that shaggy black hair and shake him for frightening her.

The arrogant tilt of his head and the flashing steel of his eyes told her he was in a fighting mood—well, so was she. "I hate you," she said simply, to deny the fiery kiss they'd shared and give him no room to take another. "I'm a top executive of a major company. I've fought my way up a male-entrenched ladder. I didn't appreciate being thrown over your shoulder and toted back to the Tallchiefs. You've embarrassed us both.''

"So you followed me for a private mauling—to keep our dignities.'' A woman who controlled her business meetings, she didn't understand the warm, dark mockery in his tone. Those smoky gray eyes slowly stroked down her body, a sleeveless cool cream linen top with matching loose slacks. In her struggle up the rugged path, she'd freed the top buttons and ruined another pair of sandals. She jerked her head away from the big hand that reached for her hair, plucking away a twig caught in the strands.

Then Liam's arms surrounded her, and he lifted her up tight against him, her feet off the ground. For a big man he moved quickly, and Michelle tried to think while her fingers dug into solid muscle and Liam's dark gray eyes stared across the inches to hers. "You like to start battles, now finish this one before you run away.''

She'd never been handled so easily, most men fearing her reaction—she could scald them with a word—but she sensed Liam would only hold her tighter and flash his heart-breaker smile. "Put me down,'' she managed shakily.

"When I'm ready. I don't like being hunted, or tracked down.''

"You knew I'd be coming after you. You could have made this easier.''

"Ah. For you to reprimand and bully me. Is that what you like to do to the men you like to kiss?'' he asked with a soft teasing kiss at one corner of her mouth. "I've told you that I'm not a game player, Michelle. You'd better leave me alone. There's daylight enough for you to make it down the trail. I advise that you do just that and keep to your pretty little life, away from mine.'' Then Liam lowered her to her feet, shot her a steely look and turned to stride through the thick grass, sending waves through the daisies and sunflowers. A distance away, he unfurled a length of cloth. The shades of blue and green caught the slight breeze that riffled his shaggy hair the color of a raven's wing. He draped the tartan around him, claiming it as his birthright, his male cloak of arrogance.

She couldn't let him get away, set the terms and tell her how to lead her life. Michelle tromped through the grass to him. She pushed away the warning sirens—a woman alone with a big strong man, aware that she was nettling him and he wasn't liking it. Oh, wasn't he? Too bad. "J.T. should have a dog and pets, and a proper yard to play in," she began.

Her anger flicked higher as Liam looked up to the jutting rock cliffs, ignoring her, a muscle clenching in his jaw. "Busybody," he murmured finally and strode away from her, making his way to the path and moving upward through the rugged forests. He moved like a hunter, body alert, eyes slashing up at the hawk in the sky.

Michelle searched the shadows falling upon Tallchief Mountain. She could safely go down the mountain and catch Liam another time. But temper and pride drove her to follow him. She passed the grazing deer to find Liam standing quietly. Intent upon a small cemetery set amid the tiny heather blooms, he didn't seem to notice her standing near. Liam looked so alone, his head bent, studying the stones marking Matthew and Pauline Tallchief's graves, the other markers, no more than large stones. She couldn't resist placing her hand on that broad back, the warm tartan covering it.

He turned to her suddenly, eyes flashing like steel, his fists wrapped in her hair. "You want to know, don't you? You want to dig into my life— Well, it isn't pretty. I don't know much. I don't know that I qualify to know who I am, because until a year ago I thought I was the son of a bitter, harsh man. I'm like Reuben Cartwright—hard clean through. And then when he died, I found a letter from his wife—she'd died earlier. He'd dragged me from a riverbank, from my parents' wrecked car and replaced his stillborn son with me.''

He flung her away, turned his back upon her and rubbed his hands over his face, the sound of his evening stubble raking in the soft night sounds. ''I don't know who I am, not really. Elspeth will help, I know—so I can pass a heritage on to my son. But inside I have too much happening now. I'm raw now, lady, and I don't understand what's happening to me up here—''

He tapped his forehead, sucked in the mountain air and glared at her in the evening shadows. ''I want to feel your breasts against my chest. To feel the scrape of your nipples against my skin, to taste your skin, to kiss you until we both forget who we are and why we're fighting…. To lay you down and love you, to burn away whatever I feel when I catch your scent, when I look into those witch's eyes. I don't feel gentle now, and I could hurt you—but I won't, because you're not driving me that far. You want to play? Find someone else. You don't belong here, any more than I do. Go back to your penthouse or estate or whatever, to your spas and servants and tennis in the afternoon at the club.''

''Beast,'' she managed too quietly and softly, rage running through her, plastered with images of Liam's big body entering hers, demanding— ''How dare you!''

''I dare. You're wanting to play, to experience a mechanic, to lower yourself on the wild side and then go back—''

Her slap on his hard jaw rang through the chatter of the night birds and frogs and crickets. Horrified that she had let her temper rule her, she shivered and found Liam's big hand wrapped around her wrist. His expression was too savage, honed by fierce need and by his anger as he tugged her to him and found her mouth with his.

She fought her needs and lost, pitting her hunger against his. She soared into wild freedom, locking her arms around his neck, her fingers diving into that thick shaggy mass of his hair, keeping him close. The rough catch of his breath hit her hot cheek, as she caught his bottom lip with her teeth.

His hands caressed a hot path to her hips, fitting her tightly against his hardened body. One hand kept her locked to him, the layers of the cloth burning between them. His other hand slid to flatten between her breasts. Then with a tug tore away the buttons.

He stilled, their heat rising in the cool mountain night, then slowly looked down at her breasts, nestled in lace against his chest. Electricity raced within her as his hot gaze—the color of steel in fire—stroked her softness and his hand rose to tear away the lace. Rough and dark against her skin, his palm enclosed her, and the ragged groan that ran through Liam's big body more than pleased her— She'd been waiting for this hunger, for this man to feed upon, a match to her own needs. Her thighs trembled against his as she placed her hand along his cheek, savoring the wildness and the gentleness of his touch. He seemed to calm at her touch; the storms lashing him eased. In that moment an unexpected softness rose in her, the need to comfort him. He turned slightly, holding her eyes, and brought his lips burning against her palm. Liam Tallchief wouldn't hurt her, not even aroused as he was now—

A methodical woman, Michelle dissected her sensuality and knew that she'd never really been open to desire, that sex with her husband was more duty than fire and need. She fought to keep balance, not allowing Liam to think he was in command when the needs ran equal between them and she could hold her own with him. She'd trapped Liam and now he was hers—

His slow grin kicked up her heartbeat and tossed it into overdrive. Liam stilled, barely breathing, his eyes locked with hers, searching— Then he scooped her high against his chest, walking easily with her through the night, across the meadow. He carried her as if he had the right to hold her, to take her, and Michelle would wonder later why she'd placed her head upon his shoulder, why her instincts told her that this moment, with this man, was right. She could trust him, give herself to being a woman for just this night.

He lowered her to her feet and, with a dark look, flung the tartan at her and took the small book from his waist, handing it to her. He walked toward the creek bubbling in the night, and she stood, the tartan in one hand and the book in the other. Clearly, she could make her decisions, and carefully placing the book upon a nearby rock, she spread the tartan upon the lush, sweet grass and sat upon it, her blood pounding and hot and her body needing—

With Liam she was alive, not the machine her parents had bred for a business wife—

"You should have gone." He came down upon her so quickly she barely had time to see the fierce look honing his face, his hands lightly shackling her wrists beside her hair. His hard body pressed down upon hers, and his desire left her aching and soft and damp. They kissed, a playing battle of lips and tongues and teeth, fierce desire awakening with the sound of their fast, uneven breaths, the heat rising between them. "You can go," he whispered against her ear, tugging it gently with his teeth.

"Or you can go. I'm staying," she whispered back, and dug her fingers into his back to lock him close.

Filled with discovery and need and hunger, wanting Liam, Michelle pushed him gently down and moved over him, holding his wrists to the ground. "Michelle—" he warned roughly. "We're going down the mountains now."

"Are we?" she smiled down at him and reveled in the sultry, hungry and frustrated look at her breasts, half-draped in the torn cloth. Liam Tallchief thought of her as a woman, not office equipment, and the heavy, thrusting desire beneath her was honest, not a rushed once-a-week duty. "I'm staying. You go. I took survival training, you know. I can manage to stay as long as I want."

He tugged a hand free to run it through his hair, his expression clearly frustrated. "Bet that cost a pretty penny, but you're not staying up here alone. It's dangerous, no matter how many fancy degrees you have."

Her summer youth camps had cost more than most people made in a year, but then it was fashionable for her group to play at hardships. Liam was pointing out the differences between them, taking control, and she didn't like it. She liked frustrating him, nudging him when he seemed too secure. "If I wanted an itemization of the differences between us, I'd have asked for it…. I have a few college degrees. I've paid some prices for choosing my career, and I could make life very difficult for you, if I tried."

His eyes flashed silver, a pulse beating in his temple, his eyebrows fiercely drawn. "You already have. Now get off me."

She wasn't ready to let him go, not just yet, and she

tugged his wrist back into her keeping, pinning him beneath her. "I'm not done with you. You can't define my schedules. Say 'uncle.' Apologize for acting like a mountainman and carting me back to the Tallchiefs, looking like a mess."

"A well-kissed mess," he corrected, easily moving his hands to lace his fingers with hers. "You liked kissing me. I could barely get a breath—"

"I haven't had that much practice. Kissing isn't a sport that I've had time for, even in marriage. I've been busy building a career, you know. Stop grinning."

The happy fuzzy feeling inside Liam was too dangerous to trust. But he couldn't let her go just yet. "Come down here and rest upon me, little witch. Stop fighting and pushing and giving directions and just let me hold you."

"I'd rather not," she murmured warily, and the husky timbre of her voice made him want her more.

"So you didn't kiss in your marriage?" he asked lightly, and knew that the question would set her off.

"On schedule, of course. We were both busy with our careers. Oliver traveled and so did I. But that is none of your business, Mr. Tallchief." The too-proper tone told him that he didn't want to know more about the bloodless tie, because what he felt now ran more to steam and fire. He didn't want to think of Michelle accepting another man, doing her duty—

"You like that, don't you? Schedules, everything neat and in its place?" Then he gave way to the playful impulse nudging him and tugged her down to wrestle with her. It wasn't a sport he'd played, but the soft limbs tangling with his were an invitation, and this time he lay over her, pinning her as she tossed beneath him. Could he trust his need to play and tease and watch her ignite?

"Say uncle," he prodded, teasing her and delighting in the flash of her eyes, the wild hot temper moving up her smooth cheeks.

"You're mashing me, Tallchief," she said through her teeth.

"Then you'd better leave me alone, hadn't you?" he asked, and regretted the gnawing need to look down at her soft, curved body pressed against his.

The next morning Michelle refused to look at Liam's station as she drove by on the only road out of Amen Flats. A busy, successful executive could always find ways of ending her vacation two weeks early—unexpected emergencies could be convenient.

She'd been bundled in the tartan, despite her protest. When she'd refused to walk, he'd packed her down the mountain trail. Shaken by Liam's easy handling when no one else had dared, she'd made her excuses to Nick and Silver and packed her repaired car. Unprepared for the stark emotions within her, she was running from a good fight, and she didn't like the taste of losing. The territory was unfamiliar and the rules too difficult to understand without stepping back for breath—for Liam had truly done that, knocked the wind from her. There were fights she wanted to win, she told herself, and ones that were worth the effort. She had a good life, molded to her needs. She knew herself. If she stayed, she'd be fighting that big, tall, hard-kissing— "If I stay, I'll throttle Liam Tallchief," she brooded as she drove out into the early-August day, sailing away to safety. "He's lucky I'm leaving."

Five

"Aye, it's good here." Liam inhaled the early-October air and cuddled J.T.'s limp, sleeping body closer upon his lap. The stars overhead seemed close enough to reach, as if his son could reach for a star and capture a dream. Camping on Tallchief Mountain seemed to be the right thing to do, with his son wrapped in the blue and dragon-green of the tartan. Liam traced the Tallchiefs' vermillion, striping the Fearghus plaid. J.T. would have this, not the cold bitterness that Reuben had planted inside Liam. J.T. would play with the other Tallchief children, though Liam found it hard to talk freely. Raised by a relentless man, Liam's life was engines and gas and tools, not conversation. He liked skimming his hand along the highland sheep's coats, thickening for winter. He loved watching his son drink pure, fresh milk and slathering butter he'd churned onto Elspeth's bread. For a time before Karen gave birth to J.T. and she had passed quietly away, Liam had tasted what a home could be, all frilly curtains and the scent of a good meal wafting through the rooms.

He closed his eyes, inhaling the scents of autumn, and admitted that he was ruled now by his emotions—and his hunger for the woman who had stirred him. She was tough, battling through his shadows to seek him out, not fearing the consequences.

He'd been wrong to lash out at her, when he wanted to cuddle her and hold her close and cherish the wonder of her body mating with his. He'd wanted to bury his face in the scent of her hair, draw that silk around him and forget the starkly cold years behind him.

He smiled against J.T.'s glossy hair. He'd loved igniting Michelle, watching the heat rise beneath that fine skin, her eyes flashing like emeralds to match the Tallchiefs' dragon-green—but Michelle was off-limits to a man who had nothing to offer.

Liam studied the flickering campfire. He knew little about women, the scary, prickly edges that had excited him with Michelle. He knew about the demand of his body, her warmth straddling him, arousing him, her breasts enticing beneath the layers of expensive torn cloth. He regretted that, the tearing of the cloth and his control. He regretted that boyish play with a woman bred to another world. She had been testing herself against a man she wanted to control—a woman in command of others, who wanted to make him ache.

Because of her, he visited now with the Tallchief family, and J.T. had been in heaven—swimming and playing for the remainder of the summer. Emily had gone to college, but now, during the day, J.T. stayed with the Tallchiefs and yelled and played and came home to sleep without nightmares. Liam wouldn't owe them for J.T.'s care, so he'd helped repair fence and machines. His taut edginess around the Tallchiefs had eased enough for him to accept their invitations to dinner. Family dinners were a good thing for J.T., seeing the love passed with the food.

He could manage the needs of his body, but images of Michelle, wrapped in his tartan for warmth, found him in the night or trapped him in the sunlight. When the breeze slid against his skin, he caught the scent of her hair, the silky strands capturing him. He wouldn't ask her to stay—she didn't belong in the small town, there were no battles to fight in Amen Flats, and Michelle was a woman who needed a good challenge to keep her happy.

The flames flickered in the campfire as Liam held his son closer. It was enough, he told himself…more than he had expected from life. After reading Elizabeth's journal, he knew more what ruled him so fiercely upon Tallchief Mountain—the need to take the woman and to make her his.

Pitch hissed, igniting in the campfire, and brush crackled as a night animal prowled. And life went on—he'd manage without that lovely witch with silky skin and hair and fascinating eyes. She'd run back to safety the next morning, away from him, and that was for the best, because one look at her and he couldn't resist taking.

At the same time, Elspeth stood on her front porch, her husband and babies sleeping within their snug home. Her parents had also been killed in October, and it seemed to be a broody month for all Tallchiefs—Liam's parents had been killed in October, and as a baby his life had changed. Elspeth wrapped her tartan around her and settled into her thoughts. The man upon Tallchief Mountain shared her ancestors, and she knew a bit of what ran in his mind—he'd set his own terms for healing and he hadn't come back to her to talk. He needed mending time and then he'd come, and she'd tell him of the family line she'd traced with Sybil, Duncan's wife.

But there was more pain waiting for Liam Tallchief. The woman who brought him to life, who clashed and fought and burned in his blood, would serve him another dark blow.

The mist was damp with secrets that would tear into Liam's new peace, a home and a journey he'd begun to make. Elspeth lifted her face to the mountain where Liam had taken his son and murmured, "When a man and a woman, equally matched, strike against each other, fire will fly—just as two flints, striking sparks off each other...."

The October rain drizzled down Michelle's office window, and she gave up rummaging through the résumés on her desk. It had been two months since her emotions had ruled her on the mountain. Liam's fierce image still churned in her mind, prowling around the lush gray office, the maroon carpet, the conference table and slid the wall of book shelves.

Her anger had surprised her later, for she had been controlled and in charge of her life since forever. A calculating woman, she had thought marriage to Oliver would suit her, too, but it hadn't. It seemed her hungers ran more to arrogant, swaggering lone-wolf men than to the gentler, civilized breed. Disgusting, arrogant, cocky, swaggering—

On the paper, Michelle drew a line with her nail. *In the dim light of his wrecker, she'd seen the red marks she'd put on his shoulder*—that fine, darkly tanned skin still taunted her fingertips, even as they stroked the desk's smooth surface.... At times, in the night, she could feel his chest against her, his heart racing beneath her hand.

Oh, there was nothing sweet in what she felt for Liam Tallchief, just the need to tear him away from the safety of his shadows—to step through the icy fortress he'd built around himself.

Michelle tapped her signature pen on her expansive walnut desk and fought the emotions running through her. She smoothed the strands escaping her chignon and thought of how Liam had held her tight, devouring her mouth—how he'd torn away her blouse to see and touch her—to fit his big rough hand around her breast, cherishing her—and the answering vibrations within her were enough to spin the earth from its axis.

She'd kept his shirt. On the fifth sleepless night, she'd given in to the need to have his scent nearby and she'd worn it as a nightshirt. She'd washed it herself, not sending it to the cleaners, because it was hers and a reminder that she could tend her own life, despite Liam's taunts.

She studied her hands, diamonds glittering on her right hand—well-kept, neat, practical-length nails, trimmed to match the one that had broken. *She'd actually cleaned house for him!*

Her lower body tightened, remembering Liam's fullness beneath her shielded by layers of clothing. He'd cost her two months of brooding, of plotting revenge and needing that harsh breath against her cheek, that heat dancing between them. If he'd acted like a gentleman later, she would have forgotten him easily, she told herself. But now he needed a lesson on how to treat a lady, and she was going to give it to him.

She moved her fingertips to the fat file on her desk and tapped them across the label, "Liam Tallchief."

Liam really shouldn't have fisted her hair and kissed

her blind and senseless on Silver's porch... "Stay away from me, lady," he'd said none too gently before pushing her inside.

Being managed like a piece of luggage went against her pride. He didn't think she could manage, that she could tend her own cooking and home. Michelle scowled at the fresh red roses and baby's breath in the crystal vase, reflected on her gleaming desk. Great. She'd acted like a woman for once in her life, had felt those deep needs and had answered them. But Liam Tallchief had picked the wrong woman to tell to stay away. Not a woman to forget a misdeed or a man's uncivil act, Michelle punched her intercom button. "Lucy, please set up an appointment with Mr. Dover."

Her boss wouldn't like his hotshot human resources director taking time off to prove that she could fit into a small town. She really needed revenge, she decided— Liam was far too arrogant and macho, and she intended to bring him to his knees, then walk away with her pride intact. "Who does he think he is to tell me to do anything?" she asked the rose petals quivering beneath her hand.

The hiss of an opening door announced Lucy, who asked with a worried frown, "Ms. Farrell, are you all right? You seem distracted lately, and bookkeeping just called with this little error—you rarely overlook mistakes. Are you certain you are all right? Should I tell the police that Theron Oswald is threatening you again? I thought he'd quit that—maybe he's been caught and put in jail where he couldn't—"

"I'm just fine, Lucy. I'm certain the police will notify us if there is anything we need to know." Michelle glanced out to the broody fall day, mist layering the streets and people on the sidewalks hunching beneath their umbrellas. She wished she were as certain as she acted. She lived in a secure building, the police had made every effort to find Oswald, and eventually she would learn to relax when her door buzzer sounded.

She didn't dismiss the danger of being stalked, but she wouldn't let Oswald's threats rule her life. She'd acted responsibly, taking precautions and placing the matter with the police. She wouldn't lead her life trapped in fear, just as she wouldn't lead the life her parents had chosen for her. She wanted a change, though, for in Amen Flats she'd found an excitement and a beckoning she couldn't ignore. It had more to do with what roamed unsatisfied within her, the need to test herself in life away from what she had known—

She'd been meticulous in her background check of Liam, tearing into his past with a vengeance after returning to Seattle. Liam wasn't the only one affected by his parents' deaths. *Was it her place to open his life? Why should she care?*

The truth hounded her: *Whatever storms ran between Liam and herself, they rang truer than her other relationships and her marriage.*

"I have a little private business to take care of, Lucy. I've requested and gotten time off to deal with it. They said to take as much time as I needed," Michelle said in her usual cool, businesslike tone, despite the excitement running through her. Liam Tallchief was no "little" business, with hot, raking eyes and a mouth that could make her— When her secretary left, Michelle sat down with her yellow pad and began an efficiency plan to remove the big thorn in her life, Liam Tallchief. She knew herself: she couldn't drop the Liam Tallchief matter until she'd put him in his place—a neat little shelf labeled Project Completed, Score Evened.

A practical woman at thirty-three, Michelle had no soft illusions about herself. *She liked to hunt and dig and find truth, and now her quest to understand more about herself led to Amen Flats and Liam Tallchief.*

Was she like other women, soft inside, needing to make her nest? Or was her heart more steel than love?

Two battling parents had seasoned her from the crib, and she knew how to survive, how to care for her own needs and pride. She liked being in control, because she'd once been helpless under her parents' manipulative thumbs. If she wanted a piece of chocolate cake, she usually ate it—because she knew the need would nag her until she got it out of her system. Liam Tallchief was a blunt, hard-spoken man and one who challenged her at a base level she couldn't resist. He'd said she couldn't cope with small-town life—she could. She'd coped with intricate, high-class, backbiting games all her life—Amen Flats' simplicity challenged her. If she wanted, for the first time, to experience more than her ex-husband's bland lovemaking, she would. She would leave Liam Tallchief drooling. The prospect was more fascinating than a corporate takeover and integration of employee benefits. "Phase One," she said crisply, drawing her yellow pad beneath the flash of her pen. "Arrange move to Amen Flats."

Outside Liam's new home, a mid-October storm growled and roared. Like J.T.'s toy dragons, sprung to life-size, the storm raged and waited to pounce. The dark clouds had layered Tallchief Mountain all day, autumn leaves slashing against the windows. His emotions were just as unstable since Michelle Farrell had soared back into town in her new red pickup. It had been two days since he'd seen her, and he couldn't stop thinking of the way her hips swayed when she'd tossed her head and walked toward him, as if nothing could stop her from tormenting him.

His hands had ached to skim those curves beneath the hug of her sweater and jeans. With her fabulous hair piled high and catching the bright autumn sunlight, she'd looked like an all-American girl—too fresh and innocent for a man raised harshly. *We aren't a match,* he'd thought, *and she's trouble.* On her second visit to Amen Flats, Michelle little resembled the expensive, do-this, do-that executive he'd first met. He was her first stop, to let him know she'd come back to prove whatever point burned her.

J.T.'s excited "Mama" didn't help as she had given him a rabbit with floppy ears and a storybook to match. While she hugged J.T. and nestled her face in his hair, Liam caught a look he wished he hadn't—as if Michelle wished for her own child, though she obviously adored J.T. When she stood, those green eyes pinned Liam, and her smile was too cool as she served him notice. "I've bought a house. I'm staying in Amen Flats."

The tilt of her chin and the set of her expression had shot him a challenge he wasn't taking. He'd been controlled all his life, and he wasn't tossing away his first peace in forever. A woman like Michelle would think little of rumba-ing all over his life and sashaying out of it just as easily.

He damned the instinct that told him when he at last put his hands on her, she wasn't leaving—

"I hope you get what you want." He'd returned giving his attention to the fan belt he was tightening. Properly taut, the belt would cause the alternator to charge, but Liam was already fully charged, from the first moment she had stepped out of the snazzy pickup, placed her hands on her hips and leveled that determined look at him.

While she'd balanced J.T. on her hip, looking like any mother, her gaze burned him, taking in the grease on his T-shirt, the holes in his jeans. "You wouldn't think that I'd be coming back for any special reason that included you, would you?"

"Kiss any frogs, lately?" he couldn't resist asking, nettled that she probably had tested those hot, sassy lips on another man.

"The world is full of frogs. It's a big pond," she'd returned evenly.

Liam drained the bath water from J.T.'s rubber alligator into the empty tub. In the two months since he'd seen Michelle Farrell, he'd picked up a rhythm to his life. He intended to strengthen that tenuous peace. Thunder rolled, the mountain storm threatening to slide down onto Amen Flats. The house was empty now—J.T. on his first stay overnight with Elspeth and Alek—and Liam ached to hold his son, to read him bedtime stories and kill the bears that J.T. suspected were in the closet and under his bed. Picking up a teddy bear that had stayed at home to comfort him, Liam walked through the modest home he had just purchased. Elderly Mrs. Akers hadn't wanted to sell, but the time had come when she couldn't maintain the house and the surrounding twenty acres. Mrs. Akers liked the thought of a boy on the tidy little ranch, and her children weren't moving back to Amen Flats. She'd decided to move in with her daughter and presented Liam with his first home at a good price.

He wanted his son raised away from customers' demands and the lifestyle that had been his own as a child. J.T. needed the backyard swing under the old maple tree, the sandpile in the old tractor tire, and flowers and grass and—Liam inhaled sharply, thinking of how he'd stripped his reserves to make the down payment on the small ranch.

The three-bedroom Akers house felt right. Though needing repair, it was filled with a sense of a loving family. Liam knew enough about repair to "make do." Everything was in place to give J.T. a permanent home and safety, and Liam could lead a smooth, day-to-day life. Just watching his son play and yell happily and grow was enough.

Everything was in place—except for Michelle Farrell, who had come back to Amen Flats. Liam came to stand at the window facing the little cottage. The summer home was built for a wealthy visitor to the mountains, who had promptly dropped interest in rural life. Liam had looked at the cottage while searching for an affordable home to put down his roots. Perched at the foot of the mountains, within walking distance of Amen Flats, the cottage was only a field away from the home he had purchased. Starkly highlighted by the flashing mid-October storm, the picturesque gingerbread trim needed repair and so did the wooden shake roof—it would be leaking now. The house would be cold, drafty from the lack of insulation and a proper heating stove, Michelle's new purchase lacked electricity and telephone lines.

Wealthy and spoiled, Michelle wouldn't know how to deal with torrents of rain washing through the house, making the rotting floors even more unstable. She wouldn't know how to keep warm—

Why should he worry? She'd come back on a whim, and he'd leave her alone. If she got too cold, she could pile into her expensive red truck and drive out of town— or she could stay with any of the Tallchiefs. She wasn't his responsibility—someone else could... He didn't want to know why she had come back, but she'd torn apart his peace from the moment she'd sauntered into his garage.

He could have wrapped his hands in that silky mass and taken the kiss that he'd needed. But instead he'd managed a cool, brief smile and returned to the tune-up at hand. If she came back for a war, he wasn't giving it to her.

Liam eased a crushed and torn letter from the thumbtack holding it on the bulletin board, decorated with J.T.'s best-colored pink cats. Raising a small boy alone prevented all tasks but those that were necessary, and it had been weeks before Liam discovered the letter while he was cleaning the wrecker, hunting for J.T.'s wind-up truck. The letter must have slipped from Michelle's bag and torn slightly; there was no dismissing the threat—"I'll make you pay."

"I keep to my own life, and she's not my problem," Liam stated firmly to himself and the memory of her kiss mocked him—

He rubbed his rough hands over his face, trying to dislodge the woman who plagued and enticed him. Romance and tenderness and eternal love may have worked for Elizabeth and Liam's ancestor, but this Liam had no illusions—his body needed Michelle's and it was as simple as that: body instincts.

And he could deny his body's needs—he had often enough—because he intended nothing to damage his life or his son's peace and safety. "She's not my problem," he repeated carefully as a bolt of lightning outlined the woman running from her pickup to the house.

Alone in the cottage, without telephone lines or electricity, she would be a perfect target for a madman.

* * *

Michelle huddled beneath the plastic trash sack. The large hole cut for her face allowed her to see the man's body outlined by lightning. In the doorway—well, it should have been a doorway, except the rotted wood wouldn't hold the door upright against the wind— In the doorway, wind whipped the man's hair and battered his jacket. Braced against the fierce impact, his legs looked as if nothing could move them—until he took a step into her house, the harsh beam of his flashlight lasering around the room covered in plastic.

"I have a gun. Don't come any closer," she said, holding up the lifter to the old wood cookstove to imitate a revolver. If Oswald found her somehow, chose now to take his revenge, there wasn't a telephone installed or security guard or a— "And turn off the flashlight—" she added, just as the beam caught and blinded her.

The rich, deep chuckle surprised her as the flashlight roamed over the trash sack around her. The blinding beam clicked off, and Liam Tallchief's dry, humorous tone asked, "Nice and comfy?"

She stood to her feet, eyeing him through the hole she'd cut in the trash sack. She hated to be caught, her incompetence spread before Liam. She'd come back to prove to him that she could manage in a small town— "I'll manage."

"Uh-huh. Come hold this flashlight while I brace up the door."

"I don't need rescuing. I'm enjoying myself. This is nothing, and I'll fix it in the morning." The steady dripping of water on top of her bag mocked her. The roof would take more than the plastic she had tried to staple on the shingles, both torn away by the wind. Unaccustomed to taking orders, she resented taking the flashlight. His low grunt didn't sound as if he believed her, and she resented how easily he picked up the door, eased it into place and dragged her small desk in front of it. She'd discovered she liked diving into the used-furniture store, the corners stacked with unique and beautiful furniture that suited the cottage. The desk needed refinishing, but she'd loved it at first sight, picturing what it would look like sanded and rubbed with oil. Maybe she had a penchant for second-hand, a new discovery about the woman who never took time to experience or to discover the beauty of old things.

Water dripped steadily into the puddle between them as Liam recovered the flashlight from her and the beam pinpointed the layers of plastic sheeting around the room. Above the beam his face was grim as he turned to her. "Do you want to talk here or at my place?"

"I haven't exactly invited you into my home, you know."

"I know. You don't like asking for help, and you don't like getting caught needing it. Am I right? Bad weather and a bad roof weren't in the tidy little plan, were they?"

"I knew it needed work. There are carpenters available, you know. I loved it. I bought it with plans of restoring it. The workmanship in the gingerbread decoration alone is unique. It's an investment and it's just that simple."

"Nothing is simple with you." He placed the flashlight upright on her desk, the beam brightly exposing the dripping and sagging ceiling. "Here. This was stuck under the wrecker's seat."

She took the letter from his hand, the crumpled letter she'd lost, the envelope torn away to reveal Oswald's threats. She lifted the plastic sack to jam the letter in her coat pocket. A practical woman—at times—she knew to keep evidence for the police. "You read it, I suppose."

He shrugged. "I saw enough. I suspect he means what he says and he'll be coming for you. The envelope was torn away and his threats were easy to see. Now are you coming to my place or are we talking here?"

Water dripped into the bucket on the floor at her feet. Her senses told her to grab Liam's strong shoulders and hold on, that he would keep her safe. But pride demanded that she call her own terms, and in her lifetime Michelle had trusted and relied on few people. She didn't trust herself now—with the need to throw herself upon Liam and hold him tight, letting his strong arms wrap around her. "I'd prefer another time. I'll check my schedule—"

He tilted his head and caught her chin with his hand, lifting her face for his inspection. "You're so cold, your lips are almost blue and you're shivering. Were you always a hardhead, wanting to have your own way, no matter what the cost to you?"

"I didn't have it easy, Tallchief. I had to fight for what I wanted," she shot back tightly.

"What do you want now?" The bald question knocked her sideways, for she couldn't tell him how badly she needed to feel safe, to have him hold her.

"I want a life," she blurted truthfully, and hated him for prying through her defenses. When Liam prowled around her, her hackles and emotions rose too easily. "I want to feel and grow things and think. I need to think and I can't do it under the pressure of running a top-notch human resources department—"

Liam's eyes narrowed. "Let me get this straight—you quit your job."

She tried not to shiver, her corduroy jacket damp. Her body's goose bumps scraped against her sweater and jeans. She didn't want Liam to see how cold she was, that she hadn't managed to take care of her basic needs.

"While I was on my leave of absence, Mr. Dover's son moved in to take over my job. Words were said, insinuations that I didn't like. I let them have the job—I'd built the human resources section into a finely tuned operation. His son can have the job without a hitch. I can manage. I've been on my own for a long time…. Okay, my priorities have changed. I want to grow flowers and paint woodwork and sand old furniture and I want to think. I've been running too hard all my life—" She shook her head, and the plastic bag rustled. "I don't know why I'm telling you all this, and by the way, where is J.T.? I hope you didn't haul him out in this—"

"My son is having a high time at Elspeth's. I called to check on him before coming here—"

"What's the matter, dear old dad? Empty-nest syndrome? Needing to scout the countryside to collect someone to push around?"

"I miss him, but he's growing up. I want him to be comfortable with them, if anything would happen to me. I want him to have someone he knows." He lifted his head to the sound of the wind tearing another wooden shingle away. "You're not staying here tonight."

Then he lifted the small desk and the door aside, picked up Michelle in her trash bag and carried her to an old battered pickup, placing her inside. "Stay put, Miss Trash Bag," he ordered before slamming the door. Through the hole she'd cut in the plastic, she glimpsed that boyish grin and wished she hadn't.

By the time Michelle had struggled out of her bag, Liam was back at the cabin, setting a plywood panel against the doorway and bracing boards to keep it in place. He hunched against the slashing cold rain and ran back to his pickup, entering it with the storm's fury and his own scent that she'd recognize anywhere.

Liam gripped the steering wheel until it creaked, his knuckles white. A bolt of lightning shot to the ground, the glow hitting his hard profile, the hard clench of his jaw. "You should have stayed away."

"I choose what I do," she answered, taking responsibility for the fiery tension that ricocheted through the battered cab of his pickup. His dark, fierce expression when he turned to her, his black hair whipped by wind and glittering with rain, told her what he wanted. Then he reached to push his hands through her hair and draw her close for his hungry, torrid kiss.

She moved toward his heat, seeking the mystery of what happened between them, how he could ignite her. He made her feel soft and strong at the same time, his unique taste too exciting to refuse. She wrapped her arms around him and her cold fingers into the warm, safe muscles beneath his jacket. He trembled against her, scooping her closer, his mouth against her temple, her forehead, her eyes and cheeks. "Hold tight," he whispered roughly as his mouth slanted to fuse to her own and her body and heart leaped to life.

She'd spent her life sleeping, she thought distantly, as his lips cruised hers, tasting and exploring and settling just long enough to torment. Now she was alive, tasting life, excitement racing through her, setting off every nerve ending; she needed to feed upon him, to devour him, and let him do the same as the rain slashed down at them...and yet she was safe and warm and— She sighed against his lips, because she knew that Liam treasured touching her, his hands trembling as he opened her jacket to draw her closer to him. The fever ran on, pulsing through her, feeding her, making her feel alive—

"Do I take you to Silver's?" he asked roughly, with just enough vulnerability in his tone to snare her heart. "Or will you come home with me?"

Six

At eleven o'clock at night, with a storm raging outside his home and in his soul, Liam rubbed his hands roughly over his face.

He'd reached out once more and claimed the woman he'd wanted. The truth of that knowledge—his lack of control—staked his work boots to the linoleum floor, his hands gripping the kitchen counter. While the Tallchief legends were based on love, he'd known little of that, and his desire for Michelle ruled him now. He shook his head, listening to the shower water stop in the bathroom. He could turn this around now, take her to the Tallchiefs and keep her safe. He'd been controlled all his life, even in making love to his wife. With Michelle, he'd stepped outside his own boundaries. But it was more than lust snaring him, it was his own reaction upon seeing her fighting the odds. He'd wanted to protect her from the stalker. Liam admired her, and the excitement in seeing her, in touching her, was only exceeded by the soft yield of her lips beneath his.

The lady had her own demands, gripping his hair with her fingers, holding him tight. No man could deny the seduction, he told himself, when her soft sigh went sweeping across his skin, the scent of rain in her hair, the silky mass tantalizing and wild and sweet, as it caught against his throat, his cheek. She'd given him insight into the tenderness of a man and a woman, the way her cheek pressed gently against his, her hands stroking his hair. She gave him ease, lying so trustingly against him in the pickup, her head upon his shoulder as they trembled with heat and desire. She kept close to him as he drove to his home and then carried her inside.

He sensed more than the moment's hot desire; he sensed he was bringing a part of his heart home to stay—

He turned to the freshly showered woman in the shadows, dressed in his T-shirt, much too large for her, her damp hair in a light froth around her head and shoulders. "We need to talk," he said, pushing the rusty words into the damp, tense air between them. "I'm not usually this—"

"Neither am I," she stated shakily, her face pale in the shadows.

Liam fought holding and comforting her, the taste of her mouth still clinging to his. "From what I read, that letter wasn't a joke. What happened? Why does he want revenge?"

Her shoulders shifted briefly beneath his shirt. "He was in the final rounds for an impressive job at Dover's. But his psychological test results were unusual. I followed a hunch and cross matched his mother's birth name to criminal records. Theron had given a false name. His real name had a mile-long list of theft...and he likes to hurt people. His references were false, and after receiving my rejection letter, he broke into my office to threaten me. It's happened before with other applicants, but nothing so violent. I had to ask the security guards to remove him and file a report with the police. It was a nasty scene. I told you that I'm very good at what I do, especially profiling, seeing if the personality type fits. I knew that unpleasant part of the job when I took it. I've done what I could for safety.''

"It's happened before?'' he asked, shocked that she'd stay in a dangerous position and furious at the nameless who had threatened her.

"I'm not a victim, Liam. I grew up with threats—veiled, but threats just the same. If I didn't want to be here, I wouldn't be. I make all the final decisions in my life. I hunt for facts, and sometimes they aren't what is expected.'' She glanced at him and crossed her arms, staring at the pattern of the linoleum between them. ''I like putting pieces together and making a fit.''

She looked directly at him now as if she wanted to say more. ''You did what you could, Liam, making a life for all of you—paying Reuben's bills, working at the station and taking care of them all, providing for your wife and Reuben. You shouldn't blame yourself for giving your wife the child she wanted. You didn't know she'd die. And some women consider that a fulfillment to know that a part of them will go on.''

"You're a woman. Do you?'' he asked harshly, as the bitter past wrapped around him and the hot water kettle hissed on the stove behind him. He briskly made her cup of tea, from the herbs that Elspeth had brought by for J.T.'s sniffles.

The answer came long after she sipped the tea and placed the cup and saucer on the kitchen counter. ''My mother wasn't exactly a model of patience and love. I'm not certain how I would be. But I know that I am not bearing the required heir for my parents because they wish it. I'm expecting them to visit, by the way, and probably cause quite a stir. It's what they do best—levy guilt and make cold, slashing scenes. Perhaps that's why I agreed to my marriage—I understood the rules. I don't understand anything with you. I've picked my place, I think, away from everyone—so the battle with my parents will be private this time. I don't want the Tallchiefs involved or hurt,'' she said too matter-of-factly, and he knew that she fought her own storms. That insight startled him.

"Have you ever looked back—I mean into your life—to see what was there?" she asked softly, watching him closely.

"No," he said, pushing the past away. "I knew what was there. Hard times and work and no money. I lived it."

"I see, but it is strange—not researching your parents or to see what family there might have been. There are newspaper clippings, church records, that sort of thing."

"It happened. That's all there was. I wanted to go on to a new life, for J.T."

She looked away, and the bolt of lightning outside his house glowed upon her frown. "So you've never gone back—really researched your family?"

"I researched enough for legalities. I saw the house they lived in." It had been too painful, opening the door to his real parents. He'd been in shock for days, holding the document, staring at it, realizing how his life with Reuben had been a lie.

"You visited the town, drove around a bit and didn't ask questions, am I right? You just took J.T. to a new life," Michelle murmured as if placing his choices into a neat, make-sense line. "You came here, because you wanted to ensure J.T.'s safety, should something happen to you. You knew you were alone, his only relative, and you studied this Tallchief family to see if they had the love J.T. needed and you'd never had. You never wondered if there could be more to your life before the accident?"

"There isn't, and you're asking too many questions that have answers too old to matter. Come here," he whispered, shadows trembling around them. He tossed away the unsettling sense that Michelle knew something more. He had to hold her again, to know that she was safe. Was it wrong to grasp for something that felt so right?

"No. You come here. I can't move, I'm shaking so," she whispered back.

When he held her close, she seemed so fragile, not like the woman who had marked him with her fire earlier. He lifted her gently, feeling rough and unsuited to the lady in his arms. "I haven't—"

Her finger pressed against his lips. "Neither have I. You won't hurt me. I know you won't. But I can't promise the same—"

He would wonder later what she meant, but not just then, with the fever burning him in the stormy night....

She hadn't expected Liam to be so gentle, so uncertain as he placed her upon his bed and came down beside her, placing his jeaned leg over her bare ones. The room was scented of him, of soap and sunshine in the sheets, and he'd had to toss aside the soft monster toy on his pillow before lowering her. Even now, lying beside her in the intimate shadows, Liam looked like a man torn apart, lines between his brows and bracketing his mouth. A meticulous, controlled man, it was no simple matter for him to take her, she realized, nor was it for her. In the mind of each, they weighed what could happen—but Michelle's intimacy with her husband had been a lie. Now she wanted the truth—raw and bold and alive, searing into her.

"Is this how you feel, really feel, touching me as if you're afraid I'll break?" she asked as his trembling hand went skimming down her body, setting it alive.

"No. I want to take everything. I'd hurt you," he answered roughly, skimming his hands through her hair, pushing it back from her face as he turned to rest slightly over her.

"Worry about yourself. I won't break—" she whispered against his mouth before it sank onto hers, forging them together. His hunger curled around her, snared her, and she dived into the sensations of Liam's uneven breath upon her skin, the warm caress of his hands, taking away his shirt.

He hurried then, in their private storm, to tear away his clothing, until his skin burned against her, fiery hot, the weight of his desire thrusting against her thigh. "Do you want this?" he whispered roughly against her breast, the tip peaked from the gentle suction of his mouth.

"I want you," she answered truthfully, for within her, she knew that she needed Liam on another level, an uncertain fragile one that could easily tear apart. But here, now, they were matched evenly in desire, hers no less than his. She tensed as his hand smoothed her thighs, as if he were exploring her centimeter by centimeter. His thumb roamed across the jut of her hipbone, circled her navel, and his hand eased upward following the line of her ribs, then up and over her breasts. His hot gaze down their intertwined bodies pleased her as it had before, the lock of heavier, stronger legs with her own too exciting for her to lie still. Her face burned with heat, but Liam's dark coloring also bore the flush of their passion.

She could barely breathe now, caught in the hot, taut storm of emotions and sensations and reeling from them. His fingers lightly roamed over her, finding her low and pulsing and warm. He stilled, trembled and she knew he fought for control, but she couldn't have that, flying off into the heat. He came to her with protection, easing upon her so lightly for a big man.

"Michelle," he whispered roughly as though her name had been unwillingly drawn from him.

She had to know, catching his face between her hands. "Have you had this with another woman—this… here…now?"

"No. Your skin is like silk—I'll bruise you…." The answer was deep, raw and filled with truth. His eyes were blazing now, his face honed with desire, and she rose to wrap around him, tethering him with her arms and legs and sighing when he entered her slowly, forcing her to wait. "Don't. You're too tight—I don't want to hurt—"

His breath caught, and above her his great body stilled as he settled deeply within her. Again that hot gaze fell to her breasts, nestled against his chest and lower to the lock of their bodies. "Yes," she whispered, knowing he waited before he took—while she could not, the fever already tightening her inside, burning…

He claimed her then, and it was just as she wanted— the claiming, the brand of his skin, his body upon hers, the rhythm forging them closer and apart. The friction of their bodies burned away doubt and left only sensations and hunger. The final pounding, riveting pinnacle came then, she against him, and he taking and claiming, the kisses rough and hungry and skin sliding upon skin as she fought to hold him tighter, her body clenching with passion.

Too soon they flew into the storm, pulsing, riding the tempest together, until Michelle heard him cry out, and stars burst in her brain and her body melted beneath his. Looking stunned, Liam studied her flushed face, her swollen, tender mouth. Then he came softly upon her, where she could hold him safe and close and soothe him after his journey.

His lips moved against her throat as she smoothed his back—that strong, smooth surface. Michelle drifted into sleep with a sense of homecoming. The erotic dream, the seductive rhythm and heat became a reality as she awoke slowly. Liam throbbed within her, filling her yet again, his mouth moving hungrily upon her breasts, his hands beneath her hips lifting her.

After the third time, later in the night, with the storm crashing wildly outside, Michelle melted warmly against him. She'd wanted—no, needed—this man to hunger for her, and his desire for her pleased her more than she could ever hope. He'd given her a truth, in his lips and touch and in the fervor of his great body. He'd waited for her, and now he was hers. "Witch," he'd whispered desperately as his body bolted deep into hers, shaking with passion. "Pretty, silky witch."

Liam stood, leaning back into the bedroom's shadows, his hand gripping the Tallchief tartan. Michelle's hair, a wild, silky mass spread across his pillow, seemed to glow, picking up the lightning from outside the window. Her scent and that of their lovemaking curled around him now. She shot deep within him, seared through the scars and the pain and the doubt to entrance him. Her body called to his now, that aching wonder that his passionate need for her would only grow. He'd had to claim her, to make her his own, and tonight they'd forged a tender bond that could haunt him later—when she saw how misfit they were.

Still, his need to hold her grew with each breath. She could raise his temper when others had failed. She could make him feel like teasing her just to delight in the emerald flash of eyes and the set of that delicate chin. Obsessed? Perhaps. He gripped the soft weave of Elspeth's tartan, the Tallchief plaid. Was this how his namesake had felt, that wild burning urge to capture and hold the woman he'd loved, Elizabeth Montclair?

Liam frowned and rubbed the ache within his chest. Whatever had happened with Michelle tonight, it burned deep within him. *He gave me two flints, the tinderbox marked with the Tallchief symbol and a love that burns true.*

He wasn't certain what burned within him for Michelle, but Liam knew it had changed his life—

Michelle stirred restlessly upon the bed, and Liam noted her slight frown as she slept. She'd ache in the morning, and it was his fault, the result of his driving need. He could give her little, of gifts and of himself. What did he know of gentler needs, the due of a woman who should be courted? What did he know of love, other than for his son?

He had to protect her from the man threatening her. He wasn't certain about the deep, dark anger brewing within him, that she'd been threatened by a madman.

Freshly showered, he breathed quietly, naked and cold in the night, the cold wind howling around his house, the past stalking on his doorstep. He'd kept to himself, but now, for Michelle, he would try— With a sense that the fragile peace and happiness in his heart could be torn apart easily, Liam walked to the other room and picked up the telephone. He called Birk and Lacey's office, so as not to wake them at the odd hour of his reckoning. It was odd, for a man who never asked help from others, to ask for Michelle, to help her with her dream of a simpler life and quickly before winter came. When Liam replaced the telephone, he found the Tallchief tartan draped across his shoulder, as if he had the right to ask of the Tallchiefs, as if he were one of them—

At five o'clock in the morning Liam slept beside Michelle, a heavy arm and a leg thrown across her as if she were his captive. She studied him, wondering who had taken whom in the tender battle last night. Later he found her in the steamy shower, those hot eyes, the color of smoke, heating the length of her body. "Did I hurt you?" he asked roughly, lifting her wrist for his inspection and kissing the fine inner skin.

"I like my privacy," she whispered through the steam, suddenly shy with the man who had filled her body and explored her as if it were his right.

"You do?" he asked with a grin that set off the flurry of delight inside her heart. "Fine. I'll leave you alone."

By the time she'd recovered her breath, the bathroom door closed behind him. She hadn't expected him to leave her alone, not after seeking her out until they were both exhausted. Nettled that he'd lost interest so soon, she found Liam lay sprawled upon his bed, stomach down, his black hair tousled and his lashes closed—sleeping like a boy without a care. She'd expected something sweeter than Liam falling asleep—breakfast, flowers, kisses and cuddling.

Yet there he sprawled, forgetting about her, stomach

down, a sheet covering his hips. She'd given him everything, and he'd taken and given back and now he didn't care? Michelle tore away the blanket and sheet and still he didn't move, breathing as if he were asleep. "Liam."

"Uh." The grunt wasn't loverlike, and she wanted her due—he could trouble himself for a kiss this morning after his demands last night.

"Liam," she said more loudly, shaking his shoulders. "Uh."

"Liam," she said more softly as she studied the length of his fine backside, the width of his shoulders tapering down to his waist, the hard muscle of his haunches. "Liam," she whispered as excitement raced through her, the need to capture and hold and take. She tossed away the T-shirt she'd borrowed and poured herself over his back, covering her own with the blanket.

"Umm," he murmured pleasantly as if coming to life when she moved her breasts against his back. "Umm…"

She nibbled on his ear. She'd never played with her husband, the intimacy now with Liam too exciting to refuse. "Wake up."

He grunted at that—not exactly a tribute to her appeal. She could have killed him then, anger riveting her on top of him. She wondered where to attack, where to begin on the huge, hard body beneath hers. She smoothed the muscles of his arms, studying the flow of her hands over his darkly tanned skin, her toes toying with his calves. He was a beautiful man to explore—those long glossy lashes, the strands of tousled hair at his nape. She kissed him there and then on one brawny shoulder and the other—

Then Liam turned suddenly, grinning, before he tugged her close to nuzzle her neck with bear growls and tickles. Amid the happiness filling her and the surprising giggle erupting into the shadowy room, she discovered that Liam was more than awake and hungry again.

Seven

"**Y**ou called them? The Tallchiefs? And asked them to help me? Listen, mister, I can take care of myself. I was planning on calling a carpenter—"

"You'll need a top work crew, not one man." Liam wasn't budging, and only the lack of a telephone in her cottage kept her from calling for help. By seven that morning, she was scowling at him. He frowned down at her, the drizzling rain outside her soggy but unique home adding to the dark mood brewing between them. The Tallchiefs would be there later, after tending their family and chores, and she wasn't in the mood for the man shaking his head.

"This house is *not* a waste of money," she said as Liam reached above her head to catch a falling piece of plaster. He placed it in a bucket already filled with water-stained and crumbling drywall. He picked up the bucket, weighed the evidence in his hand and looked at her. She shook her head, refusing to be drawn into one more skirmish about her beautiful little house, and began using a wet-dry vacuum on the floor rubble. "It's just going to take a little more work than I had expected."

"You don't give up, do you?"

"Not when it's worth fighting for," she returned honestly, tears burning her lids. She turned from him, working furiously, the vacuum sucking up her sodden happiness. She'd been so excited, eager to show Liam her dreams. She'd described the tidy little home office where she could look out on to her garden. She could refinish unique furniture on her front porch. Standing beside the hanging ferns on her porch next summer, she could wave to the warm people in Amen Flats as they passed by on the road.

"It's a doll house, honey. Built for play and not made for living," Liam said quietly behind her, his deep voice soft and slow as if he weren't used to tender logic.

She slashed at the tears in her eyes. How could she make him understand what she didn't? That her life had been led in a fast-paced lane to make money, to build a career, and now she wanted a rest— She hadn't planned to love the cottage, but she did: it filled a soft need inside her that she'd just recognized. "You don't understand."

The answer was slow in coming. "I'm trying. This place is going to take a lot of work."

"It's something I want to do, to build all my own." The words sounded childish, even to her, like a young girl defending a doll house. "Okay, me and a good carpenter."

*Okay, me and a roofer and a plumber and a siding man and a drywall man...*she added mentally. Liam's arms closed around her from behind and his cheek, rough with stubble, pressed against hers. He held her close and warm against him while the rain dripped down in front of the porch. "You look good in my carpenter pants, the cuffs turned up, and in my coat," he said finally. "You need a good pair of shoes—boots, maybe. It's Saturday morning. We could go down to the café, have breakfast, and when the stores open, I'll get you that pair of boots. I'd like to think that you're wearing suitable shoes, not something that will come apart with a drop of rain. Then I've got to open the station, and the Tallchiefs will be here by then."

Michelle turned to him, grabbed his coat and held tight. She shook him, because if there was anyone she wanted to understand, and to understand her, it was Liam Tallchief. She lied to save his pride—she could afford the price of boots better than he. "I've got boots. All I have to do is unpack them. I'm just having a bad spot, Liam. I don't need anyone to take care of me."

He eased a strand of hair away from her cheek, tested the softness between his thumb and finger. "Maybe it's time you did. I like taking care of you. Do you just like to argue with me, or is it with everyone?" he asked easily.

"You're more fun." He excited her more than any game she'd played, more than any quest she'd known.

"That's the first time anyone has ever said that. Do you really have that pair of boots? Or were you just trying to let me keep my pennies?"

"Oh, okay," she admitted darkly. "I don't have the boots—unless you mean ones to wear with long skirts. I thought I'd—"

"We had honesty last night, and nothing else will do now—for either of us. I can help you tonight and to-morrow. Emily is home from college and she's snagged my boy until Sunday night." His soft, dark-gray eyes searched her face. "You need a place to stay."

"I might. I can do amazing things in one day, and I just might have the whole house fixed by Monday."

Liam smiled tenderly and kissed the corner of her mouth and caressed her bottom, tugging her close against him. "You can do very amazing things. How are you feeling now? Did I hurt you?"

"Did I hurt you?" she returned, just as concerned, her hands smoothing his face, tracing his eyebrows and lashes and nose. Last night Liam's features had been honed by passion, his body hard and hot against hers, yet he'd touched her very gently, as though he feared to hurt her. Her hand slid down to his chest and the peak of a male nipple etched her palm, making her instantly aware of how much she liked to touch him.

"I'm a little stronger than you, honey," he noted with a slow, taunting grin. "But if you don't stop running those hands over my chest and looking at me like that, you're going to find out that everything is in working order."

His hungry, urgent kiss was enough to keep her walking on air the rest of the day.

At noon Liam stopped ordering tires and noted the Tallchiefs' pickups parked around Michelle's house. The rain had stopped, but the day was dreary and cold, autumn prowling before winter's freezing temperatures. Hammers and saws sounded in the distance, just up the lane to that little house Michelle wanted badly. She could have anything she wanted, yet she'd chosen a home badly in need of repair. Plastic covered the windows now, and Duncan, Calum, Birk and the rest were heaping lumber upon a stack to be burned. The Tallchiefs acted as a family, and they'd chosen Michelle for one of their own. He couldn't enter the family as easily, because he did not yet understand himself and the instincts that told him to claim Michelle.

Liam rubbed his neck and remembered Michelle soft beneath him, then later after the loving, grinning up at him as he foraged through his closet. Without the city suit and high heels, and in his clothing, she seemed little more than a girl—someone's sweetheart.

His sweetheart he corrected sharply, pushing away the images of another man kissing her…because her body had told him that she hadn't made love for a long time. Neither had he, and he'd been slightly rough, regretting it. He'd needed her too much, needing that hot, sweet flow of her body, her eager, hungry mouth upon his skin. Even now, hours later, he treasured her soft, sweet, drowsy sigh that had slid against his neck.

She'd worried about his past, asked questions he'd tossed away long ago. Now he tossed away the nagging doubt that there was more. J.T. and his life in Amen Flats was too good now to mar by the past.

From his station's gas pumps, Liam studied the activity at Michelle's house. Birk, the owner of a construction company, was already on top of the roof—wooden shingles flying onto the ground. The Tallchiefs could have been Liam's brothers, their coloring and build a match to his. But he'd never had a brother, and he didn't understand the lighthearted ease that flew between them. Elspeth clearly ruled them, and Fiona could pounce on one "underdog" cause or another without the slightest hesitation, bringing the family's groans. J.T. clearly adored them all. But Liam preferred to keep on the edges, where he was safe, never revealing too much of himself.

He frowned at the shouted orders, male voices carrying

in the distance. It didn't sit easily, other men taking care of a woman he had loved well through the night and morning. Then, even though it was only noon on a busy Saturday, Liam reached for the Open sign on the station door, and flipped it to Closed. He picked up the telephone to call Emily, who wanted to eat and sleep and keep J.T., but who also needed college money. "I'm leaving the key to the station at the side door. If you know of anyone who wants to pump gas until six tonight, it's hourly wages…. Yes, it's fine if J.T. stays with Elspeth until you pick him up. When you're ready, bring him home tomorrow, or I'll have a hard time reclaiming him. I'll come back tonight to close up."

This was what he wanted for J.T., Liam thought as he drove his pickup to Michelle's house—the family closeness that would hold against trouble.

He arrived just in time to see Michelle being passed out of the house, from brother to brother and on down the steps. She was shouting, threatening them all. She still wore the clothes he'd put on her, and that filled him with a dizzying pleasure—that she had kept him close.

The continuing drizzle muffled Michelle's outrage. "All I want to do is to start refinishing furniture and put a few nails in the wall, just to see how it all works. I didn't mean to turn on the water while the pipe wasn't attached. I didn't know the ladder inside wasn't to be moved and I stranded Calum in the rafters. And who would know you can't paint drywall when they're not nailed to the walls?" she demanded as Calum tossed her to Birk. Liam was waiting at the end of the line, catching her as Duncan lightly tossed her into his arms.

Lying in his arms, Michelle crossed her arms and glared up at him. "Tell them that I am an—rather, I was—a top executive and I know how to set up a concept and work with it until the product is finished.''

He adored her, Liam thought hazily as she scowled at him. She'd fight for what she thought was right, and during the night she'd pitted herself against him, gathering him deeper when he would have let her rest. A sensual woman who ignited at his touch, she filled his arms just right. He wondered then if he would ever tire of looking at her, of studying her moods. "You're pouting," he noted, enjoying the feel of her body in his keeping once more.

"Of course, I'm not pouting. I'm considering my options. They won't let me help."

Liam searched through stacks of replies, and pleasure ran through him when he managed a successful one, "They're saving the really hard stuff for you. The executive decision making. Anyone can do what they're doing—roofing, new lumber, plumbing, that sort of thing."

"You think so?" she asked dubiously, studying the men moving efficiently through their tasks. Nick passed by, shouldering lumber easily, and grinned as he took in the picture of Liam holding a steaming Michelle. A carpenter herself, Lacey had stopped by to oversee Birk and the family that had claimed her as a child. Fiona had brought by housewarming gifts of potted plants from her florist shop. The scent of new lumber mixed with those of Elspeth's stew and freshly baked bread, Talia's lemon cake and Sybil's apple pie.

Though the children were at home with their mothers now, the aura of a family filled the cottage. Liam went light-headed. Was that music in his head or happiness? Or was it coming from the sheriff's car, the Italian tenors' opera as the lawman stopped to chat? Michelle's elbow jab prodded him to answer her question. "Oh, there's no doubt that you're in charge. Your time will come. You're really the one in charge here. Ask Birk. He runs a construction crew. Hey, Birk! Michelle wants to know who is in charge here."

A man with a fiery wife who had run her own remodeling business and who had remodeled the old bordello they lived in, Birk was quick to grin and reply, "Michelle is the boss. We're just doing the basics—the no-think stuff. Hey, stop kissing her and get up here. I need a man on the other end of this job, and don't let her move the ladder again."

"I'd rather you didn't stay for this, Liam," Michelle said the next afternoon. She turned away from the expensive gray car gliding up her gravel road to the man who had carried her to his home long after midnight.

With the Tallchiefs' help the previous evening and this morning, the unfinished cottage was sturdy and dry, with a fire in the new woodstove. The windows had yet to be replaced, the plastic catching the cold winter breeze coming down from the mountains. The porch was sturdy, if not completed, and the pot bubbling on the woodstove would have to serve for meals and hot water. But with the new water lines functioning, she had running water and a bathroom—and not counting the extra lumber and sawhorses taking up space. The cottage had changed overnight and now at three o'clock in the afternoon, it was warm and snug, if not finished. She couldn't wait to choose the linoleum for the kitchen and bathroom floors, to paint the walls, and once the wooden flooring was set and varnished, she would begin carefully furnishing the cottage. She wanted to search out treasures, restore them, one by one, instead of hiring a decorator as she'd done before.

It had been an odd feeling, last night, having a man care for her, pick her up and carry her home and soap her down in the shower. Used to tending herself, she'd resented his grim care as he'd stuck her head beneath the spray, shampooing the sawdust and grime away. She'd grumbled and swatted and in the end dozed as he slid his T-shirt over her head and brushed her hair with a child's Mighty Lou Super Brush. She was already sleeping by the time he came to bed, drawing her close and warm and safe.

In the late afternoon she could still taste Liam's hungry morning kiss, awakening her with his desire. Her body still tingled and ached slightly from his, but she'd strained for release, matching him in her passion. Then they'd come back here, to work with the Tallchiefs until noon. Now, tired and alone with Liam, she'd wanted to enjoy holding him, to feel that solid muscle and heat wrap around her—

The approaching car marked the end of what would later seem like a dream—

"You'd better go now," she said, bracing herself for the two people who would tear apart her brief happiness. She expected no less from them. The rivulets of rain on the plastic and the shrouding drizzle of autumn added to her sense of disaster.

"Stop muttering," Liam said pleasantly as he smoothed the putty over the nails on the drywall.

She studied his back, the spread of his legs and his work boots locked against the rough, dry flooring and knew that he wasn't leaving until he was ready. The slow drift of his steely gaze out to the car, then back to her, leaped upon her already-taut nerves. "Liam, you don't understand. This is private."

His eyes darkened into the color of storm clouds charged with lightning. "I won't bother you. But if you think you can sleep with me, then kick me out of your life when you want, like making appointments, think again. Which way is it?"

"You're being difficult. I can take care of myself," she said finally, frantic to have him away from the scene that would become bloody very easily. Her parents usually went for her throat, and this time—so soon after making love with Liam and discovering just a glimpse of happiness—she would slash back.

"Take it or leave it," he said too softly. *Take me or leave me* trailed along his words, unsaid.

"We've just started, Liam. It's not like we're deep into a romance. Or that you have any claim on me or my life." She was desperate now, to protect him, to send him away before her parents slashed at him. She knew little how to protect a man's pride, and the rather harsh way he'd offered his help had startled her. With her parents approaching and Liam refusing to budge, a clash was certain. She could fight better alone, without safeguarding his pride and that was her parents' favorite target....

"Don't I have a claim?" he asked smoothly, reminding her of the heat between them, her need of him. She tried not to flush as she opened the door to the well-dressed, too-perfect couple that were her parents.

"Mother. Father. This is Liam Tallchief. Please come in." She shot a look at Liam, hoping he'd take the hint. She opened the door wider for him to exit. "I'll talk to you later, Liam."

"That won't do," he said too easily, putting aside the trowel and the drywall compound. He closed the new, unpainted door easily, despite her effort to keep it open. "I'm staying."

"Mr. Tallchief," her father said too coolly, in a tone that raised the hair on the back of her neck. She recognized the familiar tone.

"You're not actually going to live in this rustic little town? In this?" her mother asked disdainfully, slowly itemizing the house and then Liam, inch by inch, down his plaster- and sawdust-covered clothing to his worn work boots. "Charming." Eloise Franklin's cultured tones dripped in ice. "My daughter as a grimy workman, all that money on her education and meeting the right kind of people wasted."

Her father picked up the verbal knife and began wielding it. "After all we've done for you. You're wasting yourself here, Michelle. Only an idiot would quit the position you had at Dover's. If you knew what I went through to get you hired in any position with that idiot Ted—"

"You what?" She hadn't realized her father's connections ran to Ted Dover. She'd thought she'd gotten her position on merit, intelligence and creativity. But then Bruce Franklin never failed to strip away pride when he made his point. Stunned, Michelle began to tremble. "I worked my way into that position. You had nothing to do with it."

"Didn't I?" Her father's smirk never lied; he knew he had the upper hand and that he'd jerked her pride from under her. Bruce Franklin could prove his point, if questioned. He always took copious notes of calls—dates and times and conversations. "We're old friends. I asked him not to say anything because you're on this latest, independent tangent, and the divorce was an evident mistake. I've already talked with Oliver. He's ready to make amends and let us all get on with life in the way I've planned.''

Franklin's cold-blue eyes narrowed at Liam. "Surely this isn't a husband-replacement for the man that Oliver is—socially acceptable in our circles. Surely he's entertainment until you've finished with whatever—"

Michelle tensed as Liam's arm circled her, bringing her close to him. She elbowed him, wanting him to step away, to protect him. Liam's grim look down at her told her that he'd been in worse situations and he wasn't leaving her.

"Go away…please. I can handle this," she whispered, desperate to have him out of battle's way.

"No," he said, as if nothing could move him from her side.

"I'm used to this," she whispered again, trying to push him away. She hadn't had time to tell him—*and now her unshared secret could destroy them.*

"That's sad, but it doesn't change the fact that I'm staying put."

Her mother gasped and paled. Her father blinked as if descending into another galaxy. Then Liam checked the woodstove, banking the small flame for the night, and stuffed Michelle into his borrowed coat, as if she were a child. He smoothed her hair over the coat before picking her up. "She's tired. Call her tomorrow. The phone works. You'd better leave now."

But her father was a seasoned fighter, clearly set to battle an encroaching male. Bruce Franklin knew how to set the pegs to destroy trust. "Is this the man you've been investigating? The one with a brother who can't be located?"

The question slashed through the scent of new wood and new happiness. Michelle held her breath; *she hadn't had time to tell Liam.* She'd wanted the right moment, and in all the flurry, in the tempest between them, she'd forgotten how angry she'd been when he'd packed her off the mountain and told her to stay away from him.

A shrewd man, her father would have tracked her activities before she'd quit her job; Bruce Franklin's business tentacles were twisted and crept into corners she hadn't suspected. No doubt he knew every contact on her prized list. She thought she'd gotten that job on her own merit, on the contact list she'd built by hard work.

But her own slashed pride was nothing compared to the trust she'd broken, the pain flashing in Liam's thunderous eyes before he concealed it.

Liam's arms tightened around her, and a muscle tightened along his jaw and cheek, shifting beneath the dark stubble. Still holding her, his surprise flashed too quickly for her parents to see. Liam was a man who knew how to hide his emotions, but she knew that her father's hit had been effective. "Cut the trust," Bruce Franklin had always said. "And everything will unwind nicely to your advantage. Always take advantage. Never let emotions rule you."

Had she really lived like that? Acted like that? Without compassion, like a robot?

"Liam, I—" But the damage was done; she'd broken his trust, and, hardened by the past, Liam Tallchief wouldn't likely forgive her.

Michelle watched her parents stiffly bundle into their car; with tears burning her eyes, she wondered if she'd lost everyone who mattered in her lie, including Liam.

After her parents had gone, slamming the door behind them, Liam placed her on her feet, and ran his hand through his hair. "I should have known. They're right, aren't they? I'm entertainment—the mechanic and the rich lady out for fun. What's this about a brother?''

She'd wanted to tell him more gently, to explain that her habits were meticulous because of the careful way she'd learned to fence with her parents. But she wanted the truth between them now. ''You have a brother—Adam. I tried to locate him. He's three years older and—''

''You're right. You are good at what you do, in more ways than one,'' Liam said too quietly. She reached out to him, and he snared her wrist, pushing it away. ''I'd appreciate it if you didn't encourage J.T. from now on. Don't hurt him.''

Her blood seemed to drain onto the unfinished floor, leaving her body cold. ''I was angry with you for packing me off that mountain like so much unwanted baggage. I wanted to tell you, but—''

''You had plenty of time, lady. It's been two long nights and two days.'' Then Liam walked out of the door and drove his pickup away into the rain.

Moments later, Liam glanced at the bright-red pickup shooting like a bullet toward his home. *He had a brother, and he hadn't known all these years—Adam.*

The second fact hit Liam: *he had opened himself to a woman who didn't trust him.* From his living room window, he watched Michelle tear off his coat and, carrying it and a briefcase, tramped up his sidewalk. Her hair flew around her, almost glowing in the dreary day. He jerked open the door just as she began to shove, and she hurled into his arms, struggling free. Torn by emotions, he pushed her away.

She'd been crying and it was his fault. That thought crushed his anger and bred his guilt. He'd hurt her; he was worse than her heartless parents. He should have stayed, listened to her explain— He jammed his hands in his back pockets to keep from gathering her close.

She flung the coat at him, and it dropped aside, unheeded. She shoved the briefcase against his chest, and he held it, uncertain of what to say.

"You're just so emotional. I was waiting for the right time to tell you. Fine, be mad. Hole up here like a wounded old bear. Cover the hole of your cave door. I don't care. But here is the information I found. It's valid and it's yours. I'll refer any new messages concerning Adam Tallchief to you, unopened. I was mad when you bundled me back to the Tallchiefs and told me to stay away. I did this research immediately after I got back to my office. My father just speeded up the impact, thanks to his need to crush everyone around him."

The sarcastic bitterness in her tone reminded Liam that her father had stripped her pride—Michelle had been deeply wounded, tears not far from her when she'd learned that Bruce Franklin had set up her life. Liam placed the briefcase with information of his brother aside; he would look at it later. Michelle's wounds were new and raw, and she needed him—

She needed him. Liam breathed unsteadily, examining a new thought. He could give her something after all—understanding and patience. She'd had money but not support. He could give her that—

She turned, her hair whirling around her like a pale firestorm, her eyes flashing up at him, her expression furious. Her body tensed, her fists tight at her sides. "So we made love. Big deal. I'll live. You'll live."

"Are you leaving?" he demanded, fearing she would. She'd be alone again, fighting to survive and to keep her pride.

Her finger shot out to jab his chest. "When I'm ready…when I'm ready. I finish what I start, and I'm not done yet—uh!''

"Then finish this," he murmured after the kiss he intended her to remember. While he held her close, he kissed the teardrops from her lashes and nuzzled away the cold dampness on her cheeks. No matter what happened, she was his to protect and—the next thought sent him reeling—*Michelle was his to love.* He didn't know how to tell her, but he would try. He'd try to give her what a woman should have—tenderness and safety. "And you've got one other problem—you're not safe in that cottage, living alone. I want you here."

I want you here. The command echoed harshly through the small house, trimmed with his fear for her. In a second thought he realized that there was a whole family ready to help protect Michelle—a family who had claimed J.T. and himself. The Tallchiefs hadn't hesitated to help with her house, and all it took was one call to one message machine—no money offered and no terms asked. Liam blinked; he realized that he had everything a man could want, right here—*a family, a homecoming and a woman who had his heart were all his, after all those hard years.*

A little dizzy with the new thought, Liam suddenly admitted that all those dreams were his, the dreams he'd thought were only for other men.

He'd have to do better than ordering and yelling at her, he thought as Michelle eased away from him. Her bottom lip trembled, and a fresh supply of tears brimmed at her lids. He knew if one fell, he'd grab her close and— "I don't like orders, Tallchief. Unless I'm giving them," she stated crisply in her executive tone.

Tears and a woman's raised hackles weren't an easy

mix, and they were Liam's first trial as a man determined
to change. He ran his hands through his hair, uncertain
how to handle her, how to tell her of his need to protect
her. He'd just yelled, stunning himself, and when a man's
control slipped that much— "I can't watch my son at
night and worry about you getting hurt in the cottage, all
alone."

He frowned as another novel thought zipped across his
fears, shaking him. He'd had few allies in his life, and
Michelle had definitely positioned herself between him
and her parents. "You tried to protect me, didn't you?
When your parents arrived?"

For a moment she stared blankly at him. Then she
denied his claim with a toss of her head. "I don't know
why I should protect you. Look at the size of you, you're
strong enough to lift a small car, and you carry me all
over the place. What is that...? Carrying me? And don't
you realize how appealing you are? How good looking
and smart and wonderful with your son?"

She threw up her hands and stalked the length of the
room, picking up a toy dinosaur to cuddle it against her.
"You don't need anyone to protect you. You're so com-
plete in yourself. With those dark and dangerous looks,
that shaggy black hair that any woman would want to
cut and trim—rather like Delilah to Sampson. Oh, don't
ask me...it's a woman's taming thing for a delectable
man with hair like yours, badly needing a trim...
something about you that makes a woman want to drag
you back to her cave.... Then there's that little-boy
thing—how delighted you are with J.T. and...and those
sultry gray eyes and that arrogant swagger and those long
legs and narrow hips and that cute little triangle of hair
on your chest that leads down to—well, never mind...."

Liam fought the hardening of the anatomy she was

about to describe. If she had put her hand on him there—
But she hadn't. If she had touched him— He shook himself mentally as Michelle continued raging—"I've no
doubt that you've had women falling all over you. It just
amazes me that you've got any stamina at all, but you
certainly proved that last night—my goodness, we're
talking marathons here. I got nailed, Tallchief, well and
good. Okay, okay, so I managed my share of—I wanted
to be alive and you gave me that…whatever, and you're
trying to tell me that I would protect you? Don't think
so, bud. Not me. Uh-uh. I take care of me.''

Liam's happy little glow stunned him; his boots
seemed to float inches above the floor. Michelle's hot-
tempered opinion of his strength, looks and virility was
untrue, outrageous and flattering. He just could get used
to that sassy mouth calling him out and making him feel
like a Greek god. "I like to carry you because I'm your
lover and I'm going to be your husband and the father
of your babies, if they come along," he said solemnly,
and then gave her a kiss that was softer and spoke of the
future he wanted. "Just so you'll know," he added, when
she tore herself away from him. "You're afraid of giving
too much of yourself away, and now I know why—your
parents aren't exactly the picture of love. Lady, I'm coming after you, and I mean to win. Get used to it.''

She took a step backward, her expression set and
brooding. She tossed J.T.'s toy aside, into a toy box
stuffed with trucks. "Your son should have a puppy and
a doll—just to keep that Tallchief male arrogance in line,
and he shouldn't be an only child, either. I was and it's
rough…. But remember, Mr. Tallchief, when you start
thinking takeovers, that I make my own choices— Or
I'm going to," she said, reminding him of how her parents had cruelly interfered with her life.

"You made a big choice last night. So did I. There won't be another woman for me. I know that deep down inside. So all we have to do is to settle what runs between and you have to make up your mind what you want. It might take a while for Oswald to find out where you live if he does, and then he'll be coming for you. If you give a description of him, he'll be easy to recognize in Amen Flats. We don't have that many strangers, and he's certain to come to the station for gas. It's miles from another station. If he waits for hard winter, he'll have a worse time because of the snow closing the roads."

"Well, then. I shouldn't have anything to worry about, should I?" she said crisply, placing her hand on the doorknob and preparing to leave.

"There is one thing—" Then Liam eased her back against the door and kissed her with the hunger surging through him. "Thank you for finding out that I have a brother."

He nuzzled the soft hand that came to stroke his cheek. Michelle suddenly reached to wrap her arms around his neck, holding him tight. "His name is Adam," she repeated. "You'll find him. I know you will. You can do anything you want."

There was nothing, he thought later, like a well-kissed, soft woman, a flush on her cheeks and her eyes slightly dazed. Then his grin slid into a frown as he thought about the man stalking Michelle....

The three Tallchief brothers had brought their parents' murderer back to town, walking behind their horses. Liam wondered if he would have been so cool, if it had been Michelle who—

Pain slammed into his stomach and he recognized that the Tallchief need to keep their families safe boiled deep within him.

Eight

"**M**en." Michelle brooded about Liam as the sheriff's patrol car slid by Maddy's Hot Spot. The sheriff's taped operas were muffled by giggles and women talking. The last week of October, just one week since she'd returned to Amen Flats, was as cold as her parents' hearts. In that one week, she'd made love with Liam, and her life had flipped over—or rather her father had jerked a major portion away from her.

Her efforts to avoid Liam weren't working; he wasn't allowing her to retreat and think or brood. Since that night she'd spent with him, he was locked in her heart and in her body, her senses jumping when he was near. He greeted her with a light kiss, complimented her, no matter how paint stained and mussed she was, and he never failed to kiss her goodbye, giving her just a taste of what she really needed—his urgent hunger and the sensual storm between them. She needed his tenderness, too. As an independent woman, she wasn't certain how she felt about sharing her life.

For the first time in her life, she was under guard. Liam regularly checked her house, though he concealed that activity nicely. He brought her food and checked on her telephone service, which was miraculously installed that first morning. Liam stopped by to talk at odd times. He wasn't a chatty man, setting her suspicion alarms off right away. When her delivery trucks arrived, a Tallchief male just "accidentally" happened to stop, questioning the driver and checking the contents thoroughly.

"Amazing," she muttered, resting back in Maddy's well-worn chair. Liam's pickup was outside, and he was leaning against it. Spotlighted by a streetlight and hunched against the cold wind, he looked as if nothing could tear him away.

He hadn't run off from her parents' confrontation as she'd had other men do—especially Oliver. Liam gave no doubt that he was protecting her—and his mind-blowing kisses said he wanted her as no other man had. During those nights apart, his body called to hers—which only had the strength to flop onto her unmade bed and rest. But she still felt him—the hunger and driving heat, the trembling, shocking need that woke her from a dream of him braced over her, his features taut with desire. A woman used to controlling her own life, Michelle wasn't certain exactly what step to take next. She'd decided to run a steady course until Phase Two leaped upon her—whatever that was. Apparently, with Liam waiting for her outside, Phase One was completed.

Clearly under romantic siege and unused to being the pursued, she sipped her hot tea at Maddy's Hot Spot, and truly appreciated the sheets concealing the seminude paintings on the wall. She flicked the price tag on the plastic roses that Maddy had placed on the tables, in honor of Ladies' Night. "It's been for over a week now. I have to call Liam to let him know I'm safe, or he calls the sheriff. Can you imagine the sheriff roaring around town, coming to my house, red lights blazing, the Italian tenors singing full blast and making the dogs howl?"

The jukebox was quiet, but over Patty Joe Black's—a local farm wife—rusty, sensual blues, Talia said, "He's out there now, standing in the streetlight, waiting for you. He's worried about you, and he's getting really good at finding baby-sitters while J.T. sleeps. Liam has that dark look like the Tallchief men get in October, when they want to brawl with someone just to relieve tension. This month I wore Calum down to a nub so that he doesn't have the energy to do that. It seems like they do settle down a bit after marriage—but just every once in a while they have to beat their chests and punch someone."

"You're kidding," Michelle said, surprised at the out-and-out admission of unruly men letting off steam.

Sybil grinned. "I had to rescue Duncan from a brawl. He was enjoying it."

"Liam wouldn't brawl," Michelle shook her head and glimpsed Maddy, a beefy ex-football player and the owner of the bar. He adjusted his elastic bow tie, worn in honor of Ladies' Night; it didn't match his Play Football T-shirt. His small blue eyes widened fearfully as the local librarian began walking toward him. With the grace of a ballerina, Maddy held his tray of drinks high and moved swiftly to put tables between him and the amorous lady.

Talia placed her Hessian boots on a chair and glanced at the sign that said: "Observe the Tuesday Night Ladies' Night Rules. No Smart-Children or Good-Husband Stories. Five Demerits and You're Out of Here." "Periodically, our men like to cluster in this watering hole and mourn the good old days. It's just a matter of time before Liam joins them. Are you sure you don't want to stay with one of us, just until this is over?''

Michelle shook her head. She knew her parents well; they weren't the kind to accept her decisions lightly. She was certain they were plotting battle plans. In comparison to the Franklins, Theron Oswald's threat was a tiny scratch on a well-scarred past. "Oswald hasn't contacted me in over two months. He's probably forgotten about me. I like what I'm doing, working things out here. It feels right for me. I've got a while before I need to look for a job, and I haven't had a real vacation in years."

Amazing, she thought, how vacancies and jobs had just seemed to pop up for her as she worked her way up the corporate ladder. And now she knew why, she thought bitterly—her father was an expert at getting what he wanted.

What else did she have to do but to think and sand furniture? Her father had stripped away everything she thought *she'd* built. She'd have to pick up the pieces and see what held true. One step at a time, while she was sanding and gluing and seeking out treasures, she'd find out who she was. Along the way she would find out why she wanted to leap upon Liam every time she looked at him. He'd awakened her body, and one look at him and she felt like a tigress on the prowl. The elemental emotion was unsettling. After all, she was intelligent and well trained in social graces. After all, she'd managed employees' positions and retirements, and now she couldn't manage her life?

She surveyed the women in the room. No wonder they needed get-togethers, if managing men was this upsetting and difficult and amazing. She'd move on, fix her life, but right now the one-two punch of making love with Liam and coping with her father's shattering truth needed dissection.

Lacey snickered at the mention of brawls. "Show me a Tallchief man who doesn't push when he's on the hunt. Birk says it won't be long until Liam corners you. He rigged quite the elaborate alarm system from his station to our houses, just in case you were threatened and our phone lines were busy."

"Him corner me? Hah. I don't think so," Michelle muttered. She had to deal with her wounded pride, and Liam needed time to think. It wasn't a good combination, even with Oswald hunting her. While she tried to portray a different picture to her friends, her sources told her that someone was tracking her and asking questions. She had no doubt that Oswald would eventually find her. But she'd always met her troubles, and she wasn't running from what she'd discovered—that she had womanly instincts and that she wasn't a robot fit only for business needs. She wasn't going back to ulcer-and-stress city and being manipulated by her parents. She would keep her relationship with Liam very polite and cool, despite her hunger and need to nab him. When he looked at her in that deep, searing way, burning through her clothes to skin he'd caressed, her heart fluttered like a trapped bird.

Outside, Liam hunched against the wind and leaned back against his pickup. Michelle's blazing-red pickup was easy to spot, and she wouldn't take orders, despite the threat to her safety. She would have to ride home with him tonight, because that fancy pickup had a bit of a motor problem—just a tug of one wire ensured he had time to talk with her.

Remembering how nervous she was with him—those

pale hands fluttering to her hair or smoothing her clothes, those sultry green eyes avoiding his—was a good sign, he thought. She was still reeling from her parents' disclosure, and not certain of Liam. He had to make her certain—to hold her tight against him and feel the pulse of her body heat against his.

His smile grew as he remembered their flash-fire clash and the heat that followed. Whatever his lady felt, it wasn't the cool emotion she tried to hold when he was near. For his part he was primed and well tuned—and he had a brother he didn't know, Adam.

Where was Adam now? Years might have gone by, perhaps forever, and neither Adam or Liam would have known of each other. But Michelle had opened up the past and encouraged Liam's ease with the Tallchiefs. She was an interfering woman, a strong woman, fighting for her own life against tremendous power and influence.

Liam lifted his head, and the wind caught his hair, churning the thoughts within him. Michelle's briefcase was filled with clippings from the local paper, the wedding announcement of his parents, Tina Olson and Jamie Tallchief, followed by the births of Adam and Liam. The search for Adam had led to and ended in Australia's outback.

Ready to know everything about his heritage, Liam had taken Michelle's file on Adam to Elspeth. In the shadows of her weaving room, he followed the genealogy chart that Sybil had prepared, tracing him as a direct descendant of Liam Tallchief, son of Una and Tallchief. Liam and Elizabeth's son, Ewan had gone off to Alaska and married a Frenchwoman, Josette Benoit. Their three children had returned to the West, and Liam's father, Jamie, had married Tina.

Elspeth's mother had kept Tina's letters, and the correspondence between the two women was revealing. According to Tina's letters, the ill-fated trip thirty-five years ago was to be only a weekend, time slotted on Jamie's time off. Tina had waited until she felt strong enough to travel after Liam's birth. His parents had just discovered Una and Tallchief's story, and they'd wanted more planning the brief trip before winter. "Just a two-day hop," Tina had written. "We're leaving Adam with my mother. He's got a bit of a cold and he's cranky. He'll be fine, but this is the only time that Jamie and I can come until his vacation next year. I would so love to see Tallchief Mountain, where Una and Tallchief loved—"

Liam studied Maddy's Hot Spot and Patty Joe Black's husky rhythm-and-blues voice curled out to him. With J.T. snug in his bed, and teenage Warren Morales catching up on his homework in the next room, Liam had time to think about the woman he loved. It was strange to know that he wasn't alone, and that J.T. would be loved and cherished just as one of the Tallchief's own children. His greatest fear aside, Liam smiled. He remembered the powwow the Tallchief males had suddenly called at his station. They'd tossed him brotherly advice about handling women's prickly little edges. There was no doubt that Duncan wanted Michelle to have her due, a woman romanced properly. In an aside Duncan had asked Liam to be quiet about his concerns for Michelle. Duncan had been served orders not to interfere.

It seemed that Liam had a family, with Sybil and Elspeth and the rest cherishing his son, and the Tallchief males accepted him easily enough. "Aye," Liam said to the cold October wind, letting the warm family feeling curl around him. It was time for him to claim his love, to watch her ignite and to love her. "Aye," he murmured again, tasting the word upon his lips, and looked down at the small cut on his thumb— The five Tallchief children, filled with lore of their Native American ancestor, had originated the blood-brother custom, much to the distaste of their mother. Liam's scar was a link to their family, an acceptance; he treasured the brothers giving it to him. He narrowed his eyes, checking the cut and wondered how much sympathy it was worth. "Hmm. It might be worth a date at least."

Then he looked to the Hot Spot's front door, just slammed behind Michelle as she came out into the October wind. He knew from the toss of her head and from the way she marched straight to him, that silky mass of hair whirling around her head, that they'd clash and she'd ignite—and he couldn't wait.

Strange, he thought just before she opened her lips to scald him, and he closed it with a kiss, quickly taking the sweet hunger of her mouth into his own. Strange how she could make his heart leap, tear away his shadowy past and make him eager for the future.

They stood in her open doorway, J.T. straddling his father's lean hip. To Michelle they looked like orphans who needed claiming. Liam didn't look at all like the man who had nabbed her in front of Maddy's two days ago. He had closed her "You can't's" with a searing kiss until she'd dived in to equal his hunger. Once he'd tasted that—her need for him—Liam had simply placed her in his truck and took her to a dark lane near Tallchief Lake. They hadn't needed the pickup's heater as she'd discovered just how exciting steaming windows could be.

Now Liam stood, looking as if he hadn't touched her, ignited her, until she was nothing but a warm, drowsy smile. It was hard to refuse a man who brought his son with him, the two looking as if they needed care, with hair too long and clothes that needed tossing away. She knew that J.T. had better clothing, because Liam took good care of his son.

He gave her a grin and his son to tend, kissed her and closed the door behind him. What chance did she have, Michelle wondered, as she helped J.T. take off his coat. The little boy's eyes widened as he looked around to her paint cans and the old table she'd been sanding. Michelle's heart tilted precariously. She wanted to gather him against her. She wanted children, as simple as that, and she knew how Liam's wife had felt—the need to give him a family, a child, a part of herself.

Liam entered her house, stirring the sawdust in the room as he carried in long poles. He glimpsed her rumpled bed in the other room, and his gaze seared hers. The image of his long hard body intertwined with hers leaped into her mind. "Daddy, can I tell her?" J.T. asked excitedly. When Liam nodded, J.T. rushed to explain. "My daddy made you something. It's to make quilts to keep you warm. It was my idea. Elspeth's mommy had one, and she sewed in the winter when she couldn't play outside. I want to hide under the blanket you make like Elspeth and Fiona did under their mommy's."

J.T.'s growing need to have a mother like the other children became stronger every day. "You can be my mommy, if you'd like. We'll adopt you, just like the puppy I'm getting from Mrs. Rainey. She says that Calum's Olaf is the daddy. He's big and shaggy and my daddy says he'll eat more than he weighs. I get to feed him. If you came and lived at our house, I'd let you feed him, too."

Liam shook his head, clearly surprised by J.T.'s unusual outburst. "He used to be a quiet boy.... It's a quilting rack. You can lift it up to the ceiling when you're not working on it. Fitting quilting pieces together seems to fit you. We brought you a basket of old clothes to practice on, though you'll probably want new material.'' Liam was busy fitting the poles together, J.T. hurrying to help, kneeling to hold the wooden sticks.

''It's a perfect gift.'' Michelle's throat almost closed with emotions. She'd had a sleek apartment, push buttons to make life easy, but she'd never had anything so thoughtful. ''You're right, J.T., I do like to make things fit. I'm going to enjoy this, and you can come play under it while I sew.''

''No dolls. Just trucks,'' J.T. stated firmly. ''You have to sew pieces together, before you use this. My dad says so.''

They looked so perfect together, father and son bending over their task, that she couldn't tell Liam of Oswald's latest threat. Over the telephone lines, his voice was shrill and chilling, raising the hair on her nape. And he'd hurt anyone who got in his way, he'd said. She could manage; she'd always managed her own life. She would keep Liam and J.T. safe by leaving Amen Flats and just the glimpse of happiness she'd had. For tonight she would imagine them as a family, warm and safe. She'd give herself to cuddling J.T. and Liam's sweet, seeking kisses. She'd stuff the happy mix into her heart as a memory.

But it was time for her to go—and she knew exactly what to do to protect Liam and J.T. and the family she adored. Her life had been a lie, created by her parents. But she was good, Michelle decided firmly, not allowing doubts to sway her. She couldn't doubt herself now, not in this, when it came to hunting Oswald. She'd find him and put him away. Meanwhile, she had to leave Liam and J.T. She couldn't bear to think of Oswald hurting them. There was only one safe way to keep Liam away—

Michelle's letter was harsh and cruel and didn't ring true. Her handwriting was uneven and stained as if tears had dropped upon the linen stationery. Liam held her letter, the words telling him that their "moment" was over and that she was bored, ready to move on in her life; small towns weren't for her. The bitter surprise had been waiting for him when he stopped by her cottage before opening the station. J.T. was already at Sybil's, eating her blueberry pancakes as if starved and waiting for the television's morning cartoons.

Liam looked out into the frosty morning and knew that he couldn't let a part of his heart fly away so easily. He picked up the telephone and dialed Sybil, asking her to mind J.T. until he returned. His son wouldn't mind the time apart now, secure as he played with other children. His hand still on the telephone, Liam noted the light blinking on Michelle's message machine. "I know where you are now," the man's voice hissed. "I watch you every day, and you're going to pay for ruining my life."

His blood chilling, fear making his hands tremble, Liam telephoned Abe McDonald who always milked his cows early and who lived near the only highway coming or leaving Amen Flats. Yes, Abe had seen Michelle's flashy red pickup, but much earlier, when he'd come out to check a sick cow. She'd been driving fast, and the sheriff had pulled her over, his "danged" operas making the hounds howl. Abe's wife had awakened and she "gets real cross without her sleep." Abe sternly informed Liam that he needed to "keep better tabs on your woman."

"I intend to." Liam's next call delighted Warren

Morales, who could pump gas after school. Shaking his head, Liam called the elderly woman who had applied for a job to help her pension money. Sara Fay Jenkins wanted daytime duty and informed Liam that she would clean up the garage, too.

Twenty minutes later Liam drove out of Amen Flats. In rural Wyoming, there weren't many main highways, and a city woman wasn't likely to take off into the farm roads; she'd want the driving ease and the convenience of gas and food and shelter. Liam trusted his hunting instincts, and prayed he was right. In his two hours of driving one hundred miles on the highway, several service station attendants had confirmed she'd passed by in that "snazzy" red pickup, and she'd asked one of them where was the nearest motel. Liam spotted Michelle's pickup parked outside the motel room. Heart pounding, fearing that Theron Oswald had already— No. No, he wouldn't think that way. The clerk didn't question that he was Michelle's husband, needing another key, or her lover, meeting her on a rendezvous. Jamming a flower bouquet under his arm, Liam didn't knock; if Oswald was in the room, surprise was on Liam's side.

Inside the room Liam breathed quietly, listening to the sound of the shower. On the desk Michelle's laptop was open, patterns of words running down it; paper slid from the miniprinter. Someone was feeding her information, expertly tracing Oswald.

Liam placed a Do Not Disturb sign outside the door, then tossed the bouquet aside—his first apart from those he'd brought Karen when she'd given him J.T. Propped up with others at the last gas station, the mixed-flower bouquet reminded him of Michelle—sweet, complex and fragile, easily crushed. He wanted to go into the bathroom, hold her tight and know that she was safe. He prowled through what he could say, how to say he loved her, and every thought dropped away as she stepped out of the bathroom, clad only in the towel knotted at her breasts. "Liam!"

He tossed her letter upon the bed. "Nice. What about J.T.?"

Her face was pale in the shadowy room, her fingers trembling as she pushed back her damp hair. Outside, on the highway, trucks roared by, but the sound was quiet compared to the beating of Liam's racing heart. Michelle spoke quietly, her husky tone uneven. "I thought I'd send him toys."

"Toys won't cut it. Did you think I wouldn't come after you? Did you think so little of me that you didn't trust me?"

"You know why I left."

"Yes. I know you're tracing Oswald. You could have done that in Amen Flats."

"I didn't want him near Amen Flats. He won't stop at hurting others, not even a child. I know his profile…what choices he's likely to make. A friend, a former police officer, is running a check on stolen credit cards now on the computer. According to Ray's information, Oswald prefers a certain victim—young, sweet with a purse filled with credit cards. He likes to watch their faces fill with fear. He usually leaves them where they can't report the loss until he's used the cards. Once Ray pinpoints Oswald, and I have enough proof, I'll turn everything over to the police."

She punched his shoulder and wiped away the tears shimmering in her eyes. "He's after me, and he'll hurt anyone close to me. Don't you think I love your little boy? Don't you think I love you? If anything happened to either—"

"You love me?" he asked harshly, looming over her, his eyes the color of steel.

"Don't let it go to your head, but yes. I'm not certain I like it. I like neat plans, and since I've met you, nothing has been neat and scheduled. I thought I'd deal with the immediate danger, get myself far away enough to protect you and J.T., and once you're safe, I'd—"

Liam took off his coat and tossed it in a chair. He sat on the bed and bent to unlace his boots. "What are you doing?" she asked as he propped himself against the headboard.

"Watching you get all lit up." He crossed his arms over his chest and studied her too intently, that slow dark gaze warming her beneath the towel.

"This is serious, Liam. Oswald means business." As she did in her office, she paced the room. She tried to ignore the way Liam tilted his head to study the towel barely covering her bottom. She braced her hands on her hips and frowned down at him, jerking aside from the big hand that reached to stroke the inside of her thigh. Liam knew just how to distract her. "How did you find me?"

"A pickup like yours is hard to miss around here. Since the last gas you got was at my station, I knew you'd have to stop. I just asked questions. But I would have kept looking until I did."

"I thought my note explained everything quite clearly," she stated with an imperial sniff that sent most men running. "I'm bored. I'm moving on. Get out of my life."

"Are you now? Then you shouldn't have told me you love me. You can't just throw a thing like that at a man and tell him to get lost." Liam tugged lightly on her towel. Only a slightly civilized tether kept him from tearing it away. He wanted to tell her with his body—because the fine words wouldn't come easily to him—that he loved her. "Sit down and let me brush your hair before it tangles too badly."

In a gesture he'd seen before, Michelle threw out her arms and issued a frustrated feminine "Aargh!" The towel slipped, unfurled and Liam tumbled her into his arms. He moved over her, holding her squirming body beneath him, his hands shackling her wrists. He could no more stop himself from kissing her than he could stop breathing, and she met his hunger with her own, just as he knew she would. Then he looked lower, to the softness tipped in peaks he wanted to taste. "Tell me about that love part again."

Michelle trembled beneath him, her eyes dark-green as the currents ran between them, sizzling the air. Her hips thrust up to his heavy desire, just that once, that telling single time, and when she licked her lips, the jolt shot straight down to his need. "There are maids outside the room, Liam. It's only ten o'clock," she whispered shakily as he cupped her breast and brought it to his lips.

Michelle cried out, twisting and heating beneath him. Yet he asked, because he wouldn't force her. "Do you want me?"

He had to know, to salve his torn emotions, that she wanted, that she needed him. If only like this, in the wild brew of soft limbs and sighs and pulsing heat. He had to fit himself to her, tearing away his clothing, but only after her kiss told him she wanted him as desperately.

"Yes, but I'm going to regret it. You can't just take me this way—look at me with those wonderful gray eyes, as if you can't think of anything but me. It goes to my head, and I can't think straight. I'm a cool-thinking businesswoman, Mr. Tallchief. Do you know what that does

to my ego—to know that I want to toss you on the ground
and have you?''

He laughed outright then, joy racing through him. ''I'll
let you take me the same way. Fair is fair.''

''You're cocky, Tallchief. Someone needs to bring you
down to size.'' She ran a fingertip across his lips, and he
caught it with his teeth. They were breathing hard, holding each other tight, not ready to give just yet.

''That wouldn't be you, would it, Ms. Farrell?'' *The
flint and the fire,* Liam thought, and knew he'd never
been so alive. One spark could set them off, but more
than that ran between them—something that would last
when the fever had burned low, a tenderness that would
have them holding hands at ninety.

Right now Liam had to deal with the fever, the fire
between them. She tossed her hair, and he wrapped his
fingers in it, letting her know that he wasn't letting her
get away easily.

''You're going to be insufferable, but I'm letting you
get away with it this time.'' She flung herself at him, that
soft, sweet surrender of her flesh gathering him close and
tugging him deeper. She was glowing now beneath him,
tossing against him, pitting herself against him. Her
hands ran over his back, anchoring him close. He locked
his hands beneath her hips and gave himself to her, cap-
tivated by the tightening rhythm of her body. He fought
to keep hold, to tell her that he loved her, but with the
last of his strength he managed to ease down beside her,
holding her close.

Her head on his shoulder, the scent of her shampoo
and shower blending with their lovemaking, Michelle
was already asleep. He cuddled her close, smoothing her
breasts and back and down her hips. Just the feel of her

in his arms made the world right, to know that she wanted him and that she was alive.

"I'll kill him. I'll wrap my hands around that beautiful thick neck and I'll strangle him—" He'd left her with a tingling deep within her, the laziness of being well and quickly loved. The new pair of boots he'd given her were perfect for tracking him. And he'd taken her printouts, leaving her nothing, but a note telling her to "Stay put. L."

Well, he had left his Tallchief tartan and a snapshot of him holding J.T. "Beast," she muttered, fighting for breath and fighting his pickup through the gears. He'd taken her automatic drive pickup, and with the Do Not Disturb sign on the motel door, she'd slept for hours.

In the late afternoon, the mountain shadows were already sliding across Amen Flats, and first of November air was so cold she could see her breath as she tramped up the mountain path. Agnes Morefield had said she'd seen Liam earlier, hunting with the Tallchief "boys" up on the mountain.

The path twisted and led upward, and Michelle panted and plotted what to do with Liam every step of the way. She grabbed a bush, hauling herself up a small embankment hand over hand. She glanced at the deer leaping from the woods, Tallchief Mountain soaring cold and high above her. "Fine. He wants to play games. I can do that. I can't believe he left with Ray's printouts, that he actually left me. Not after I told him I loved him. There should be a certain amount of consideration after that declaration. I question his status as a gentleman."

She slung the woolen tartan around her shoulders against the cold, the fine mist gathering on her hair and clothing. Only her anger kept her going now, the sound of a dog barking high on the mountain—the shot seemed to shake the rocks beneath her feet. Her knees almost gave way, and Michelle thrust out a hand to grasp a tree. "Liam...."

The moon slid behind a cloud, and the path was more difficult to see. Yet she hurried—Oswald wouldn't care who he hurt. "Dear Lord, don't let Liam be hurt...."

The white shadow running toward her wasn't a ghost, it was Thorn, Duncan's huge hunting dog. She wrapped her hands in his pelt, avoided his licking tongue and ordered, "Find him for me."

But Thorn was running away already, and tall men moved toward her as the clouds cleared the moon. She couldn't move as the Tallchief men came closer, shoving Theron Oswald none too gently ahead of them.

She searched and couldn't find Liam, then suddenly he was beside her, looming over her. "Looking for me?"

Michelle couldn't move, and when she could, she flung herself at him, burrowing against his chest, holding him tight. Liam's hand held her face against him, where the solid thud of his heart told her he lived. She grabbed his ears and pulled his face down to kiss him. He wrapped his arms around her, picked her up until their mouths were level and met her tiny kisses with his own. Between kisses, he whispered, "Hush, Michelle. Don't cry, honey. It's all over."

The Tallchiefs moved past them, men bred to hunting and protecting their families. Oswald's shrill threats caused her to turn, to push Liam away and confront the man who had threatened her. One good kick in his shins wasn't quite enough, but with Liam holding her, tugging her back to him, she couldn't get in a really— "Just one punch. Just one really good punch."

"Aye," Duncan said, a man who'd experienced a hot-tempered woman set on revenge. "We'd better get Oswald to safety before she tears him to pieces."

Then because the Tallchiefs moved on down the mountain, Michelle turned to Liam and punched him solidly in the stomach. His grunt and surprise eased a little of her terror and panic. "There. I had to use that somewhere. Remember that the next time you leave me at a motel."

"Now, honey," Liam said uncertainly, rubbing his slight injury. "There was only one place he could be—close enough to see everything that went on. He'd bought binoculars, a high-powered scope and rifle and camping gear."

"So you just took it upon yourself to call your family, and all you wonderful, strong men went after him. What was that shot?"

"Oswald's rifle accidentally discharged. Everyone is okay." Liam caught the ends of the tartan around her shoulders and brought her close to him for a long, sweet kiss. "Aye, I do have a family. It's not a feeling that I take lightly. We came here alone, J.T. and I, and now he's so happy. I called the Tallchiefs and they came. No questions. They know the mountain better and I wanted no mistakes. If Oswald got away, he'd be more dangerous than before."

"You made a wise choice. They've hunted in these mountains all of their lives. Thorn has been on more than one manhunt. But you could have been killed. Make love to me here—now. Let me know that you're alive."

His sharply indrawn breath caused her to step back. The hand she'd slid beneath his coat came away with a warm stickiness—blood.

Nine

That night, for the first time, Liam had the unique experience of being pampered by a woman and berated at the same time. He also had the odd feeling of being very cherished and very much in danger. He'd been ordered to lie on her bed and not to move. He wasn't certain about anything, except that for the moment he'd better do as she directed. The superficial burn of the bullet across his side was an excuse to groan periodically and stop Michelle's current tirade. She had run to his side, eyes wide with concern, The flurry of soft kisses across his face had distracted him from his earlier terror that she could be hurt. He glanced at the bedside clock, a feminine little thing on tiny feet, and realized his woman had more endurance than he'd suspected. His love was a strong, strong woman. She had forced him to lean on her down the mountain. Admonishing him while she undressed him, she'd cleaned the wound. She'd put him to bed, and she showed no signs of tiring.

He wanted to hold her, make love to her and cuddle her while they slept. And then he wanted to make love to her again.

"Don't you dare move, Liam. You're not leaving my sight, not after leaving me in that motel room. I had to have a mechanic put back the thingamajigs you'd pulled apart, and your pickup is like driving a board—no power steering."

Michelle crossed her arms beneath her breasts, and her satin robe parted above her thighs to reveal lacy black panties. Liam had blinked when he'd first seen them, the erotic need to place his hands on the fine lace and smooth it away to the soft flesh beneath.

She turned, tapping her toe as he lay on the bed, and presented him a view of her rounded hips. His body was aching now, and not from the searing bullet. "So, you took my pickup to let Oswald think I'd come back, so he would stay put. Then you and the rest of your clan played posse…. Without me. The one who got the reports in the first place. Here, lie still and take this aspirin. I'm not finished yet. You're staying in that bed all night— J.T. was asleep hours ago at Elspeth's. Oh, no. Don't you move. I'll tie you down if I have to. Let me check that bandage. And one more thing, you are not going to work tomorrow."

"Are you going to cluck all night? Or are you coming to bed?" Liam muttered and tried to erase the sight of Michelle's breasts, clad in a satin robe, hovering over him. The fine perspiration on his forehead wasn't from his wound; it was from watching Michelle undress after she'd tended him. It was from feeling her hands search his nude body to see if he'd been hurt anywhere else—

he'd edged away from those small, curious hands as they'd sought injury on the inside of his thighs.

"Well. Of course, I'm coming to bed. And you're going to lie very still. And in the morning we are going to the doctor—oh, no. I'm not listening to any grumbling-old-bear sounds. I want to know that the wound isn't infected."

When Michelle turned out the lights and settled into bed, Liam lay very still. He was, for the first time in his life, aware of how cold a big soft comfortable bed could be…. How cold and rigid looking the shoulder of a woman could be when turned away from him. He smiled later in the night as her hands found him again, stroking his chest, smoothing his hair. Drowsily he realized that Michelle had tied his wrist to her bed. The bit of lace could easily be torn free, but he wanted to see what she intended. Other than that, his ego needed the boost and her scolding reassured him—it was nice to think of himself as Michelle's valuable property. A man she intended to keep.

She bent to whisper in his ear, "You're not leaving me tonight, Liam, so go back to sleep."

"I'm right where I want to be," he whispered back, and took the liberty of stroking her thigh.

She pushed away his hand, adjusted the blankets over his chest and flopped down, to turn her back on him again.

He wondered who had the most endurance. At the moment his was questionable, and Michelle was in a substantial lead.

"Are you all right?" she asked before dawn, leaning close to him, her breasts nestling to his side.

"No," he whispered against her kiss, and sucked in his breath as her lips moved lower, kissing his chest.

"Honey, you've tied one of my hands," he reminded her. "I'd like to put them both on you."

"You can do very well with one. I'm not letting you get away while I'm sleeping," she returned, sitting up in the shadows to tug away her robe. The look back at him over her bare shoulder made his heart leap into high gear. "Do you hurt very badly?"

"No," he whispered as she gently, carefully eased over him, taking care to stay away from the overlarge bandage she'd placed on his side.

"Don't ever, ever do that to me again, Liam," she whispered, bending to kiss him in a way that took his breath away. She rocked gently upon him, her bent thighs tight against his, her hands braced against his chest. Still wary of her tirade, he took her movements for a good sign. The caress of her voice gave him hope. "Oh, Liam…"

Her hand slid between their bodies and found him. When he could think later, he would remember the exquisite feeling of being captured and cherished as she slowly took him into her body. "Don't move. I don't want you bleeding again. Let me," she whispered.

Careful of his wound, Michelle moved slowly, finding the rhythm that they both needed, her body tight upon his. There in the shadows, upon her bed, with her body burning his, he forgot everything but his love for Michelle.

"I'm not J.T.," he grumbled in the morning as she called the doctor for his appointment. Preparing for his shower, he'd shaved and tucked a pink towel around his hips. The color upset him: pink was a color he associated with women's clothing.

Michelle replaced the telephone in a very exact gesture, as if she were preparing a logical defense. "I'm aware that no one has taken care of you and that you resist change, Mr. Tallchief," she said coolly.

She turned to eye him, the November sunlight sliding over her satin-covered breasts. He could almost taste her skin, hear those wispy sighs passing over his skin, but the images died when she turned to frown at him. "I'm not happy with you. I'm going to cut your hair—stop grumbling. Someone has to take care of you. Then we're going to the doctor's office. I really do not like being this emotional. It's uncomfortable. This will take time, Liam. Imagine…stranding me in a motel room while you charged off to defend me. That won't do."

Liam rubbed his jaw, nicked by her tiny razor. A small piece of toilet paper, used to stop the blood, fell into his hand. Apparently women could hold a grudge and still make love as if a fever consumed them. Liam wondered why women had to be so complicated. All he wanted to do was to love Michelle. "You're talking like I'm an employee who needs a reprimand."

"I'm talking like a woman who will not be pushed around at your whims."

He lifted a brow, challenging her. "Someone had whims last night."

"Oh! Oh! You'd bring that up now? You who left me in a motel room? Who—"

"I've got a headache, dear," he managed to say more quietly than he felt.

"That's because your head is very, very big," she said too quietly. "And you look ridiculous with those little bits of toilet paper all over your face."

"I had to shave with a very small razor," he returned. Liam noted that part of his body did indeed feel very large and uncomfortable, the towel taut across his hips.

Waking up to a woman brushing her hair in the nude, all the soft supple curves gracefully flowing with her movements had been jarring. Her bedroom was very feminine, done in ruffled curtains and an old claw-foot dresser, bottles and pictures arrayed across the top. She'd bent over to rummage through a chest, and his body had instantly lurched to life. The sight of her hips shimmying into the skimpy lace briefs was enough to make him sweat. She'd shocked him, too, because he didn't know average women wore such inviting underwear. Stripteasers, maybe—the thought had rocked Liam, and he realized the bed wasn't vibrating—he was.

His son's picture had grinned at him from a miniature gold frame, making Liam uncomfortable. Aware that this morning had presented many first experiences, Liam decided that he would retreat to think, to ponder upon how a woman could make love to him and in the next moment point out all his misdeeds. Showering in Michelle's tiny fern-bedecked bathroom with an array of delicate bottles on the vanity, he felt as if he'd stepped into a fragile fairy world. The mirror labeled his dark, hard features as an intruder. He ran his hand over the hard-packed ripples on his stomach and flexed his muscles, in an uncustomary estimate of how he physically appealed to Michelle. Liam Tallchief—stark, tall and heavily muscled—amid the feminine, rain forest decor and lush soft pink towels. What did he know of scents and soaps and the silky negligee hanging on a bathroom hook? Just inhaling her scents caused him to ache. Liam shook his head and realized how fragile and susceptible he really was when Michelle was near. He ripped away the pink towel covering his hips. With Michelle he had to deal with his own emotions, and he wasn't certain what they were now.

The staunch hatred of Reuben had eased somewhat.

Liam had realized that life had more to offer than the bitterness of the past.

His son was evidently happy and well settled, and Liam's fears that J.T. would be left alone—should something happen to his father—were gone. A legal document provided that Elspeth and Alek would care for J.T.

Michelle had brought tenderness into his life, a sense of belonging in the community and a family he cherished.

His boyhood dreams had come back, that of owning a small farm and raising a small garden.

But with Michelle came hurt, too. She'd been stripped of her pride, and she was questioning herself, who she was. She didn't trust him enough to share those fears.

He had to give her more, Liam decided. And he'd have to find a way to be more gentle with her, to say the things she needed to hear. From Elizabeth Tallchief's journal, he glimpsed what women sought—a gentleman, something that Liam had never been. He decided to study Elizabeth's journal more closely, to see how he could romance Michelle.

Waiting for Michelle was not easy. Nor was living separate from her.

"Here," Michelle said later, holding up the white shirt he'd given her at the lake. "There's blood all over your other shirt, not that it's worth saving."

"Stop fussing. I feel like I'm J.T. off to the first day of school. I can't wear this. It smells like a girl." He sniffed at the feminine scent on the collar. But he did wear it, just because it pleased him that she'd worn the shirt, thinking of him. He held very still while she moved around him, smoothing the shirt with her hands and inspecting him. He had the unique and dizzying feeling of being cherished.

* * *

Once she was certain Liam wasn't too badly hurt, Michelle told him he'd better keep his distance—a reminder of when he'd told her to stay away.

"Can't," he'd said after following her to Tallchief Lake. In early afternoon, the cold winds swooped down from the snow-capped mountains, foretelling winter. "You'll catch cold if you stand here too long."

"I'm used to taking care of myself. I'm still mad at you for scaring me so badly."

"Think you'll get over it?" After her scolding, Liam was beginning to suspect that he loved a woman with real endurance.

"Not for a while. I don't even know who I am, Liam, and you're confusing the issue."

"That's good," he said, and stood looking at the dark, brooding lake with its whitecaps. "You know me well enough. Do you think I'd fit into one of the Tallchief legends?"

"Of course. No question about it. You're the stuff legends are made of. Think of all that you've done to keep J.T. safe and ensure his future and give him more than you had. That is more than honor, that is dedication and love. But I can't get over the sight of your blood on my hand and how you deliberately put yourself in danger. I can't think when you're around, and I've got my life to settle. I've seen women jump around in their lives, never knowing who they are. They enter a new situation before they finish the old. I won't do that. *I have to know…and I'm so angry with you now, that I can't think straight.*"

"Well, then. Since I'm in trouble anyway, I might as well—" Liam tugged her into his arms and slanted his lips against hers. His kiss was long and hungry, his desire rising against her through their clothing. When she was shaking—and not from the cold, but from the burning

inside her, the need to have Liam fit his body upon hers—
he released her. She resented her weak knees and wondered frantically where one made love in the wild.

"Just a little bit to tide me over…while you do your
thinking. Put that in your schedule."

That evening Michelle replaced the telephone to her
father's long-term secretary in Seattle. Now retired, Sally
Alden had always been dedicated and truthful—and
Michelle had loved her. "I told your father it wasn't
right, setting up your life," Sally had said. "But yes,
that's just what he did, pulled strings, bargained, whatever he had to do. In an odd way, I think it was his way
of taking care of you, of seeing that you didn't have to
work as he and your mother did. They didn't have anything but love when they married. And then they had you.
They picked your ex-husband, Oliver, when you were
only ten. I think that was their way of providing for you
after they were gone. I'm sorry that didn't work out."

"I'm not," Michelle muttered as she settled in the old
rocker Liam had given her. He knew just how to get to
her, to bring her something so precious, needing care.
The gift was a sturdy, lasting piece of someone's life that
had been cherished, and most certainly babies had been
rocked to sleep by loving mothers in the very place she
sat.

Michelle remembered being rocked as a child and how
her mother had held her close. She remembered the scent
of her father's aftershave; he'd tickled her as he held and
rocked her. With Liam in her life, it was important to
mend the corners of her life. She could do no less than
he had, and she would try—but her parents had to do
their share, too.

She settled down to rock and think, the creaking sound
of the chair and the crackling in her stove the only sounds

in her small house. She picked up the old clothing he'd given her, to practice her quilt-piece cutting. She studied his old shirt and then hugged it to her, taking comfort from the scents of J.T. and Liam. If anything had happened to him—

"Women." The second week of November passed without Michelle's snit easing. Clearly, while his son had her attention, Liam was in the proverbial doghouse. It was a very cold place after Michelle's big warm bed. It was four o'clock on a Saturday afternoon, J.T. was building blocks at Calum's house, and Liam was dreading his empty bed. Warren and Sara Fay were at the station now, arguing over the fine points of the coming car wash. They'd close the station for the weekend. Liam ought to be thinking about a Saturday-night date with Michelle, how she'd look, what she'd wear and how the evening would end with her in his arms. Instead he was finding comfort in the family who had taken him in as one of their own.

In his lifetime, Liam had missed brooding with other males, trying to understand the intricacies of the female mind. Just yesterday, when he was lying on the floor at his house, playing with the new train track J.T. and he had built, he'd turned to see Michelle in the kitchen. She'd brought a casserole and stood in his kitchen dressed in a red sweater and long, tight jeans. Holding the casserole with pot holders, she'd stopped to look at him, poised in the kitchen light. The look she'd given him reminded him of the hot, sultry one when she'd loved him that night—as if she wouldn't finish with him until neither one of them could move.

Liam sipped his iced tea, served in a beer mug at Maddy's Hot Spot and continued to brood. Michelle had waltzed into his house, loaded with packages. She stripped off her coat, hugged J.T. and let him help her unpack the new clothes for them. A dark-green icy stare at Liam had told him to keep his distance and not to mention anything about repaying her. He would somehow, but clearly then wasn't the time. While the washer chugged and the dryer whirred the new clothes, Michelle and J.T. had gone to work on the closets. "Mama needs scraps," J.T. had chirped happily, shoving old clothing into a sack. "She's making me a blankie with all my favorite clothes in it."

"How's it going?" had seemed to be a safe remark for Liam. From her icy look, it wasn't safe, and The Motel Incident wasn't forgotten.

Liam ran his hand over the scorch mark on his shirt. He'd thought Michelle's ironing at his house, arranging the new clothes in his closets was some kind of woman-therapy thing. He decided not to mourn all those fine old clothes, just broken in right. Or to offer to pay for the clothes, though keeping silent went against his pride. He'd given her that rocking chair, needing refinishing. He'd hauled it up to her doorstep and plopped it down, resenting his need to see her. Nothing would do, then, until she had him put the rocker in her house, move it and move it again, for just the right place. But when she gathered J.T. upon her lap and tucked her chin against the boy's black hair to rock, her expression held him.

Liam recognized the emotion—holding a small soft child gave comfort in troubled times. A child gave hope when life was dreary. Michelle battled her identity questions and her pride by herself, keeping Liam apart. He'd sat in a chair and just watched her, the creaking of the old chair the only sound. If his body weren't in a continual ache, those moments of sheer peace might have been enough—just watching her rocking his child and finding comfort.

Peace wasn't in the life of a man who had offended Michelle, he decided, as she opened the door to Maddy's and stood outlined in the neon lights. Her hair was loose and wild, just as he liked it, and the fire in her eyes leaped immediately to him. He settled back to watch her, Elizabeth's legend running through his mind—*When a man and a woman equally matched strike against each other, fire will fly—just like two flints, striking sparks off each other. 'Tis a game, finding the strength of a man and challenging that truth....*

Was that how Michelle felt, needing to come after him? Needing to clash with him to test what rang true between them? Or was he romanticizing and praying that all that fire held more than temper?

She could have left town at any time, but she'd preferred to pump her own gas at his station, wipe her own windshields and then glare at him through the glass.

A man was delicate before the tricky elements of a woman's mind, Liam decided warily. The heavy thud of his heart told him it had nowhere to run, because she held it in her palm.

Michelle stalked toward him, the boots he'd given her clumping on Maddy's wood floor. The silver earrings he'd given her flashed and swayed amid her hair. They weren't the professional style she'd worn when she first arrived. They were inexpensive, delicate filigrees that whirled and turned and fascinated, warmly dotted with carnelians.

He'd taken J.T. to select them from an old man high in the mountains; Liam had wanted his son to know the mountains his ancestors had loved. The old man's work was intricate despite his gnarled fingers. The Tallchiefs

understood family, the old man had said, eyeing father
and son. "You'd be a Tallchief, all right. If you're doing
your courting with my earrings, I'd say you're determined. You brought your boy, too, teaching him the ways
though he's just a tike. That's good, to hold family close
and give them what you know. I have something here
that I've been holding a good long time. It belonged to
a Tallchief woman, too. Elizabeth Tallchief she was. She
got a new loom and gave this one to my great-great-
grandmother.''

When Liam had given her the earrings, Michelle had
said, "They're lovely.'' Then the tears had come to her
eyes, dark as the dragon-green of the Tallchief tartan.
''That's really how you see me, isn't it?''

''I see you as yourself. Strong enough to take what
comes and meet the future,'' he'd said honestly.

''They're so feminine—not my usual taste. They're
rather flamboyant for me,'' she'd said thoughtfully. For
a moment Liam had been frightened that she'd be offended with his choice. Then she'd said, "I love them.
Thank you.''

She'd kissed him, placed the earrings into her lobes
and studied the mirror intently. "Yes," she'd said quietly
as if agreeing with his choice. "I think a change is good,
don't you? But I still haven't gotten over you leaving me
in that motel.''

Standing between his spread legs now, leaving no
doubt as to who she'd come to see at Maddy's Hot Spot,
Michelle tossed a paper on the table. Recognizing a
woman on the warpath and glad that it wasn't their
women, the Tallchief men immediately excused themselves, deserting Liam.

He let his gaze roam over her dark-rust sweater, a
match to the carnelians in the earrings, down those

curved hips and long legs sheathed in jeans. Little kept him from reaching out to smooth that feminine line or to tug her onto his lap. But after days of uncertainty, Liam needed some comforting reassurance that Michelle cared.

"That's the police report," she said in a businesslike tone, as if her lips hadn't run hot and silky beneath his own, as if she hadn't sought him in the night. "You keep forgetting that I'm thorough. You underestimate me. The report is worse than I thought. You *did* endanger yourself. Oswald had held everyone at gunpoint. You included. You leaped at him. You actually threw yourself at him so the others wouldn't be hurt."

"All I want to know is if you're done bossing me, and if you're tromping out of town still mad at me, or are you staying?" His tone was surly, but a man without a sense of how to handle his woman had the right to be growling. She stood firmly between his spread boots, and the image brought back the one of her easing over him, capturing him—Liam inhaled sharply. "I'm not begging," he added, just to keep his pride. "Make up your mind."

Her eyes narrowed. "I always do. I wouldn't think of leaving. I'm not finished with you yet."

He grunted, the primeval noise suiting his instincts to carry her off to his lair. He wanted to ravish her and be ravished in return. Michelle was a woman who matched him in passion—hot burning passion that he hadn't experienced in over a week. "Figures."

Michelle left, stalking out as she had come in, the view of swaying hips drying Liam's mouth. The territory clear, the Tallchiefs returned to the table, sprawling around it and grinning knowingly at Liam. "Shut up," he said pleasantly, because one could do that to men who were almost brothers.

"Shut up, yourself," Birk returned easily. He plucked a pink baby rattle from his flannel shirt pocket and waggled it. "I guess we'll have to retract your title, 'Liam the Lover.'"

"Give me advice I can use or leave," Liam ordered sullenly. He mourned that smooth, cool control that gave him shelter from hot-blooded women.

"Hey. We just stopped by to help you lick your wounds," Alek said.

"You're in the doghouse, boy, and first base is a long way away. Better ask her for a date," Maddy stated around his well-chewed cigar. "But whatever you do, don't act like those other Tallchiefs when they had woman trouble. Don't start a brouhaha that might cost me a mirror."

Nick rubbed his forehead. "I hate it when women think. You never know what's coming—it's like a cocked gun."

"Well, she's doing plenty of that," Liam brooded. "She's holed up there, stitching little pieces of material together and rocking by the window. She's playing with J.T. during the day and tucking him in, and he's calling her 'Mama.' I'd like to make that a legality."

"Silver says no woman would like being stranded in a motel like that," Nick offered.

Oh, well, Michelle was all woman, Liam brooded and noted his rough hands. He glanced at the Tallchiefs and wondered what they used on their hands. Their women liked to hold hands.

Big Sam MacIntire, a bully from another town, chose that moment to burst through Maddy's doors. His construction crew grumbled about layoffs, and the men lined up at the bar. "That was a cute little number who passed me on the way in. Curvy with green eyes and long hair down to here. Looks like a real handful, too, top and bottom, like she'd keep a man busy—''

The hard scrape of Liam's chair as he stood should have warned MacIntire. It didn't. He didn't take the hint when Maddy hurried to cover the big bar mirror with a hard foam panel. Big Sam still didn't take the hint when Liam's big hand caught his shoulder and spun him around.

An experienced brawler and one who had been at the wrong end of the Tallchiefs when he'd pushed them, Sam narrowed his eyes. ''What?''

He glanced at the tall, lean Tallchief men, now married and somewhat tamed, as they settled back into the shadows. Sam knew he'd have to fight fairly or they'd jump into the mix. The cool stranger looked like the Tallchiefs with his black hair and gray eyes and hard features. He looked as though he'd seen a few hard times and needing a trimming.

''Maybe you'd better leave,'' the new Tallchief invited too quietly. A muscle flexed across his jaw, and in his eyes was the look of thunder and lightning.

One assessing stare down the relaxed but powerful set of the Tallchief's tall body and Big Sam knew he had a good, fine match. ''I'll bet you shave with a woman's razor,'' Big Sam said, just to start things rolling....

The sound of crashing glass caused Michelle to close her pickup door, the one she'd just opened. She had plans to copy Pauline Tallchief's quilts, making small cardboard cutouts for piece patterns. She needed Elspeth's company after seeing Liam sprawled across a tavern chair, brooding at her. Her hackles up, she knew that little kept Liam from tugging her down on his lap. He had that raw, hungry look that only fueled her need to pounce on him.

''Don't you dare!'' she ordered sharply inside Maddy's

as a burly man drew back his fist to hit Liam. The man was bigger, a belly bobbing over his belt. The cut over Liam's eye dripped with blood, and the other man's eyes were swelling, his lip cut.

She didn't have time to ask the other men for help. They were obviously commenting on brawling techniques. She had to save Liam. Scowling at her, Liam's attention was on her when she saw the man release the punch. Liam crumpled to the tavern floor.

"I told you not to do that," she said to the man as he leered at her. The bully wasn't Oswald for whom she'd trained, but she did a neat enough job that the man sagged back against the bar, trying to catch his breath.

Liam struggled to his feet and sagged back, elbows propped against the bar, scowling at her. "What are you doing?" he demanded, as if she'd broken a rigid male law.

She reached for a napkin, dunked it in a pitcher of water and dabbed it across Liam's cut. Like a sullen little boy, instead of the tall powerful man he was, Liam jerked away, disdaining her care. She loved Liam's dark, edgy moods. She loved walking straight into them and seeing what happened. "I was just evening the odds. Your relatives obviously won't help. They're all grinning over there, but they won't be when I tell their wives. You're outmatched. He weighs more than you. And you are not a fighter, Liam. Leave that to the rest of the—"

She aimed a pointed look at the Tallchief men, who had not bothered to help Liam in his time of need. They had the look of men gathered together for protection.

"He's slow. It was just starting to get interesting," Liam muttered. "If you'd marry me, none of this would happen."

Michelle stared at the man she knew could be gentle and kind and loving. "You're coming home with me,

Liam Tallchief,'' she said between her teeth. ''Where we can settle this in private.''

She marched out the door, missing the boyish grin Liam shot back at the Tallchiefs. She also missed their thumbs-up signs.

She'd had a rotten day, brooding about calls from her ex-husband and her parents. With clouds looming low on Amen Flats, she'd searched for long distance consulting work she could do while repairing her life and staying in Amen Flats. As she had expected, her father's tentacles had blocked her nicely at every turn. Those job-hunting calls emphasized how much of a pawn she'd been—all the while she'd thought she'd been chosen for positions on merit. In the end, exhausted by thinking and remembering, she'd helped elderly Joe Tomlin stack his woodpile and clean his house.

There wasn't anything more exciting than nabbing Liam Tallchief, Michelle decided. Liam had that all wound up, raw and fiery look she loved to ignite. Michelle heard Liam's heavier footsteps follow her up her porch steps. She wouldn't look back at him, wouldn't let his sheepish look derail her. ''Brawling,'' she muttered, noting the tarp covering a mound on her porch.

She'd opened her door, the warmth of her woodstove greeting her, before she walked to the tarp and tugged it away. The wooden cabinet of the old, treadle sewing machine needed Michelle's sanding and oil, but Liam had repaired the black metal head, scrolled with gold leaf. The bird's-eye-wood sewing cabinet beside the old machine needed work, but it was good and solid, topped by a rubber dinosaur. The big wooden hoop was just what she needed to keep her stitching taut on the quilt designs she'd made. And a tiny wooden chest, marked by water, sat on a crudely fashioned bench. A huge, disassembled, and obviously old, loom was propped against the house.

Michelle turned to Liam, her heart leaping. He knew perfectly well how to touch her heart, how to make her want to leap upon him and place hurried kisses all over his hard face, just to watch the tenderness soften him. "What's this?" she asked, wanting the words from him, not just the gesture. He had to meet her halfway in what brewed between them.

He looked off to a field filled with Appaloosa, as though wary of her reaction. "Sara Fay Jenkins has decided she isn't sewing anymore. She's tuning carburetors and taking a course in new car mechanics. The other things are Mrs. Akins. She had them stored in the shed and wanted you to have them. J.T. wanted you to have a dinosaur for protection—living here all alone without us."

"I love them. I'll take very good care of them. J.T.'s dinosaur will sit right where he can watch any threat," Michelle murmured when she could speak.

Liam reached into his pocket to extract a small, brown-paper-wrapped parcel. He opened the twine and slid the earrings into his big, scarred palm. The green stones gleamed against his dark skin. "J.T. picked these. When the jeweler asked me the color of my true love's eyes, I said they were green as grass, dark as a high mountain meadow in summer rain, warm as the love I have for her."

He watched her intently as if fearing the impact of his words would terrify her. She could only take the earrings, lock them in her fist and hold them over her wildly beating heart. Liam stood there in the chilling November wind, looking as safe and solid and unchanging as Tallchief Mountain. The wind brushed his hair, and when it lifted hers, he reached to smooth it. "My true love," he repeated softly as if fitting the words to his lips for a lifetime. "With eyes of dragon-green and lips as soft as a rose petal."

Michelle tried to catch her breath. No one had ever spoken so to her. This man could reach inside her and make her melt with words, a look or a touch. "Do you really feel that way?"

He nodded curtly, apparently unnerved by his own words, his emotions running deep. "Wouldn't say it if I didn't mean it. And maybe someday, when you're over that motel incident, we can go back there—after we're married...if you'll have J.T. and me."

"I'm still working things out about my career. I don't know who I am just yet."

"I do. You're the woman I love. You can do whatever you want about your career, it won't change how I feel about you. And I think you know just exactly who you are, but you haven't fine-tuned the works just yet."

"You're not asking anything—" she whispered, loving him. "No terms?"

"I'll be honest...I'd like you in my bed, if that's what you want," he said flatly. "That's about it. Just so you know that hot storm you stir up inside me with those eyes and that mouth isn't exactly sweet...then there's this—"

Liam opened the wooden chest for her to see. "My namesake, Liam, gave these to Elizabeth and now I'm giving them to you. Duncan and the rest want to give me something of Tallchief and Una's, and maybe when we're settled, you would choose for us both. Those pieces of wood against the house are Elizabeth's loom. Una taught her how to weave. Properly set up, the loom is a big thing, so you might have to add a room here. Or I'll build one at my place. It's your choice. Take your time thinking, honey. I'll get better at this as we go along."

Ten

The silver car glided up the road to her house, threatening Michelle's joy. She'd just discovered how susceptible she was to Liam's new facet, the tender words of a lover and the look of a man who would last through the years. Michelle took Liam's hand and tucked the earrings in his pocket. "Keep these safe for me, and I want to hear those fine words then, too. Don't forget the 'dragon-green-eyes' part. Shut my door, Liam. I don't want them in my house just yet. They have a way of tearing things apart and I'm not ready for that."

"You're doing just what you should be, honey," Liam said quietly. "You're mending your life. I'll understand if you need to leave, to do what you must do. But I'm hoping that you'll always remember me."

"You can take it then, the battles we'll have? Because you're not an easy man, Liam, and you set me off. I used to be quite the cool businesswoman, you know."

"We've both changed, and as for me, I like to see you get all wound up and steamy. I used to dream of owning a ranch, you know—when I was a little boy."

"You did?" She looked up at him and wondered when he would ever fail to surprise her.

Her parents slammed the car doors and stared at her, obviously hoping she'd be the first to reach out. When she held Liam's hand tightly, her father scowled and took her mother's arm, coming to Michelle's steps. They looked up at her.

"Take it easy, honey," Liam murmured. "They are the only grandparents our babies will have. If there's a chance they can change, I think you can train them. It's your decision, not theirs."

Her father wasted no time. "I see you haven't begun to pack. We can send movers. Most of your things are still at your place in the city."

"I'm staying." Michelle didn't know how life would turn and twist for her, but she knew she'd do it at Liam's side. Her parents would have to accept her terms this time, no strings attached. She wasn't certain they could do that.

"It's just a phase, Michelle," her father said. "Like when you were ten and wanted to go camping by yourself. You'll get over it, and what's that pile of junk doing on your front porch?"

"He's been in a fight. And you look very—" For once Eloise studied Michelle carefully as she stood beside Liam. Eloise was very quiet, and then she took her husband's arm. "We're leaving now."

"But...but..." he protested.

"Look at her, dear. She's blooming. That's how I used to look at you. Time will tell. Come along now. She's a fighter, just like you, and she'll make up her own mind how she lives her life—just like you. They look like a team, standing there like that. Just like us. And I've waited long enough for a grandchild. He'll do nicely, if he's what she wants. I'm certain she's got everything in control, scheduling his life and theirs. Don't push her too far, Bruce. Think of it as the point of no return in a business deal.''

Michelle met her mother's tentative smile with her own, her heart warming because she knew that her mother was beginning to understand. Healing would take time, but that soft, shared smile between them was a good start.

After they were gone, Michelle turned to Liam who was studying the old furniture, scowling fiercely. She held the small chest tightly. ''It's not junk. I love it. And I won't get bored. You're far too exciting. How long do you have until you pick up J.T.?''

''Just long enough, and you're coming with me to get him,'' he said, picking her up to carry her into her house.

He kicked the door shut and eased into the rocking chair. He'd dreamed it was big enough for him to hold her and J.T. and maybe the babies that would come along. He'd awakened hard and aching after dreams of Michelle moving over him on that fine old chair. While daydreaming of how she'd look and feel, snuggled on his lap, rounded with his child, Liam had overfilled a truck tank. For a man raised to hardships, daydreams were new, enticing experiences.

Michelle opened the small chest and prowled through the contents. ''Obviously old and treasured. A tinderbox, a battered straw, a man's ring—oh, look, it has the Tall-chief symbols!''

She carefully unwrapped the two flints. ''Rocks. Chipped. Wrapped in fine old velvet. Liam, this obviously means something.''

''The chest was found with me. You'll have to find out

what the rest means. You like putting pieces together."
He loved how she looked, fiercely determined, turning the
flints in her hands, trying to see into the secret they held.
Elizabeth's legend had been right—Michelle and he had
struck sparks from each other, and they'd ignited a love
that would last forever.

Michelle closed the chest carefully and placed it aside.
"You'll tell me now, or else."

In one of those quickly changing moods that always
would fascinate Liam, she smoothed his cheek. "You've
really left the past behind, haven't you? I mean the way
Reuben took away what you could have had all those
years? And Adam?"

Liam held her closer, settling back to rock his love in
his arms. "I'd like to meet my brother. I think with you
helping, it's a scheduled event. No, I'm not thinking about
how it was growing up, the stripped life and foraging for
myself. I'm not wasting more time thinking about a hard,
bitter, selfish man. I have a new life with you and my
son.... And you're the cause of that, dragging me out of
that rut, making me see that life held more. I think I'm a
better father to J.T. because of you, and if you hadn't come
into my life, I might not have known about Adam."

He kissed her forehead and rested his cheek against
hers. "Think of what you've done, honey. Breaking away
from the past. That's no small thing. Or working to un-
tangle years of interference from your family. Think of the
difference you've made in my life, how I can feel as if I
belong with my family now. That's what I wanted to give
J.T. most of all, a family. I feared that he'd be left alone
and raised by someone as uncaring as Reuben. But he's
safe now. And what you've done for yourself, making a
home away from anything you've known—few people can
do that. I've no doubt that when you decide you want to

do a task, you can do it. I'm hoping you'll let me share your life, though.''

"You're not getting away from me, and you know it, Liam Tallchief," Michelle said quietly, sitting upright. "I've found what I want, right here with you. All the excitement and challenge and what I've wanted all my life. Whatever else comes, it will just be that much better. You make me *feel,* Liam. I like feeling like a woman, feeling needed and cherished, and I accept your offer of marriage. There will be terms, of course. In short, Mr. Tallchief, you've been bagged.''

"Well, not quite," Liam murmured, and caressed her lightly just to watch her get all steamy.

"Mmm," she said thoughtfully, tilting her head to study him. "I think I do that well, too." Then she stood and began removing her clothing on the way to her bedroom.

"No ruffles in our bedroom and no pink towels," Liam stated as he stood next to her, the shadowy room enclosing their bodies, clothing tossed aside.

"Mmm," she murmured thoughtfully again as if she had plans of her own, and moved into his arms. She held him close, before the loving, resting against him as she was meant to be. Each touch treasured and heated, until Michelle jerked her head away, looking up at him with those green, green eyes. Liam smiled briefly, his body ready for hers; they'd clashed, and sparks had flown, and now came the fire. He reached down to that soft bottom, cupped it and lifted Michelle carefully, until her legs wrapped around him. He took her lips, tasted the wild hunger of her tongue, the heat within her, and then found her breasts, soft against him.

She cried out, her body aching for his, the tug of his mouth sharpening her desire. Her fingers dug into Liam's marvelous wide shoulders, anchoring him to her for a lifetime. She had no time to tell him of her love, not just now, when their bodies' needs must be met. "Hurry."

He lowered her onto the bed, her legs still wrapped around his hips. Then they were one, his heavy body resting over hers. His fierce expression told her that this was no light moment, that it was a bond of bodies and souls that would last forever. His hands caressed her hips, trembling, to tell her that he kept her safe, not allowing his passion to run wild.

She smiled against his lips and bit him gently. She couldn't have Liam banking all that fire, not now. There would be other times when love would run gently between them. His big hands caressed her thighs, the fever burning within him. Oh, how she loved to see Liam ignite, all that cool drop away. She loved the way his dark-gray eyes studied her flushed face, her lips that he had kissed. She had to taste his body, to lick his nipple and suckle to set him off.

Then Liam came down upon her as she wanted—hard, demanding, hungry. She met the thrust of his hips with her own, met his mouth and tasted him as hungrily, aware that her need came purring from her as she stroked his back and soothed and took. There it was, she thought distantly, reveling, touching the man inside, the man she loved. The flames came tearing into them, bodies locked and moving slowly, surely toward the summit. He gathered her closer in that tender struggle, his mouth burning her flesh, skimming a path to her throat, nibbling and foraging until he treasured her breasts again. The edge of his teeth, not hurting her, set her off, riveted her as he gently suckled and nibbled and kissed. The clenching of her body rushed on, beyond her control. Texture on texture, male and female, sliding erotically into passion, his breath warm against her skin, caressing and heating and cooling and sensitizing—''Liam!''

Liam went taut over her, his huge body throbbing, just at the same time she cried out, reaching for him as the stars burst. Held tight on that pinnacle of pleasure, she let him bring her safely, gently back to earth. She could always trust Liam, she thought, patting his wonderful backside, to provide surprises that delighted her.

''Not quite yet,'' Liam murmured as she dozed, and he began to give her another world-shaking, best-ever surprise.

Later they picked up J.T. and went home for supper and television. Sensing excitement between the adults, J.T. wouldn't settle for anything less than Michelle reading him a story. Michelle fell asleep on J.T.'s bed, and Liam thought he'd never seen a sweeter sight. In the morning they were off to Duncan and Sybil's for Sunday-morning breakfast, and the day passed all too soon. Then J.T. badly needed his bedtime and Michelle once more fell asleep while reading a story. They were still asleep when Liam left to open the station.

On Monday evening Liam sighed ruefully in the manner of a man who hadn't had time to cherish his ladylove. He took his after-work shower and tried to do the station's books. Young Morales and Sara Fay were quite a team, taking the chore of ordering tires and other inventory needs.

Michelle had J.T. for the day, the boy reveling in the woman he'd captured to read him nighttime and sometimes daytime stories. Though Liam had been quite careful to keep his son's life based in their home, J.T. had adapted to visiting his cousins. Not long ago he could not be taken from Liam's side. But J.T. made it clear that he wanted

"My own Mama, not someone else's, and I want her," he'd said pointing to Michelle.

"The old woman-capturing game," Liam murmured, aware that his son and his namesake shared a tradition.

Then Michelle's red pickup pulled into the driveway, and she walked up to the house, wearing a large overcoat and the boots he'd given her. Inside, she watched Liam intently. "Where's J.T.?" he asked.

"We're picking him up later at Nick and Silver's. I forgot something when you were at my house the other day and in my bed."

"Oh, what was that?" he asked, bending to take her lips, a taste he'd needed all day.

"To say I love you." She opened the coat to reveal nothing beneath but fully curved, soft woman. And from the look in her eyes, Liam knew life would never plod along again.

"So does this mean I'm finally going to get a date?" he asked, settling in to enjoy her reaction. He enjoyed teasing Michelle, if he could keep his eyes off that luscious pale geography beneath her coat. The crest of her nipple caused his body to jerk and tighten; the curve of her hip and those intriguing shadows above her thighs caused his mouth to dry.

She tilted her head back and studied him with those fascinating dark-meadow-green eyes. "I still don't know the meaning of those two rocks in your wooden chest. They're obviously precious. I asked Elspeth, who seems to know more than anyone, and she just smiled and referred me to you."

"You'll have to work on that one, won't you?" he asked, not letting her have her way so easily. Elizabeth Tallchief's words coursed through his mind—*'Tis the game, finding the strength of a man and challenging that truth.* He had his own game, and Elizabeth had provided a badly needed insight on women—his ladylove in particular.

"Oh, I will. You know I will, and I've got a lifetime to work on you, Liam Tallchief," Michelle murmured as he bent to untie her boots.

Finished with the task, he ran his hands up her smooth thighs and eased off her coat. "It's enough, then, for you? Life with me and J.T.?"

"More than enough. I think I loved you from the first moment I saw you framed in your doorway, trying to do the best for your son. Now are you going to pick me up and do that marvelous carrying-off thing, or not?"

"Aye, I will and I'll never stop, rose of my heart." With delight he watched Michelle's dark-green eyes widen, and he began to laugh. There was nothing more exciting than stunning her with the words that came straight and true from his heart.

On a mid-December afternoon, Michelle ran her fingertips over the old journal on her lap. In Liam's home, as his wife of two weeks, she settled back for a few moments of peace, rocking in the big chair by the fireplace. Liam and J.T. had mysterious father-and-son missions now and were away for the afternoon. The spacious new room added onto Liam's house was perfect for a small family and scented of new lumber. Shadows drifted over Elizabeth's loom, assembled in a corner by the window, J.T.'s toy train-set on the floor. Michelle loved to hear Liam laugh now, that chuckle that said his life was rich with love, and that she had given him ease. Then the wonderful nights, long after J.T. slept, when they would toss upon the bed, challenging each other, the fever too hot to wait.

At other times the loving was gentle and sweet, telling each other of their love.

Outside snowflakes swept across the small farm Liam had always wanted, and the big basket on the floor beside her was filled with her own dreams—a garden and ideas for more remodeling. For inside Michelle nestled a new life, so new that it was only hers alone—she wanted to be certain before telling Liam. She wanted to reassure him with a doctor's verification that she was in good health and ready for children. Liam's dream of growing things would come true, and not only vegetables and animals, either.

Michelle sighed, drifting in the peaceful moment. Helping the high school counselor test graduating students for their aptitudes was exciting, placing young lives on a path best suited for them. The women's shelter offered another challenge, helping unfortunate women straighten their lives and provide for themselves, helping them retrain for suitable jobs. Every day was filled with excitement, the hunt for Adam intense. From the facts they had gathered, Adam had apparently walked out of his hometown as soon as he could. He left no forwarding address, and his share of the inheritance had been left in an attorney's safe keeping. To all appearances, Adam Tallchief did not want to be found. Liam's parents' and his grandmother's estates, had gathered a vast, unused, bank interest. Proof of his legal identity would place half in Liam's hands, yet he'd wanted to wait for Adam.

She frowned slightly, thinking of Liam's mysterious and somewhat boyish mood, the secrets he kept from her. Michelle studied the small chest on the fireplace mantel. She still hadn't discovered the meaning of the two rocks, but she would. Then, as if the woman from another century called to her, Michelle opened the journal and began to read.

* * *

An hour later Michelle hurried up Duncan's steps, the two flints captured tightly in one hand and the tinder box in the other. She dismissed the other Tallchiefs' pickups and rapped at the door. J.T. swung it open. "Mama!"

"Hello, my little man. Where's your daddy?" She would leap upon Liam the first moment she had, tear him to pieces. He'd made her wonder and pry and question and held her away from the truth.

J.T. pointed to Duncan's living room where all the family had gathered, dressed in kilts and tartans. Elspeth fussed at their hems and broaches while children squirmed in their arms and toddled around their legs.

Liam scowled at her, and her mouth went dry as she stared at him. Dressed in a ruffled white shirt, a tartan sash and kilts, Liam was gorgeous. All rugged, untamed male, his features fierce in a scowl. He looked just like what he was, the descendant of a Native American chieftain, clad in a tartan as a reminder of Una, the bondwoman. "Now, you've done it," Liam said flatly.

"Me? I did what? You're the one who kept the secret of the legend. But I know now, Liam Tallchief. I know what the flints and the tinderbox represent. Watch—" She bent to the fireplace, arranged straw upon a stone and struck the flints together. A spark leaped onto the straw, igniting it. "That's us, isn't it? Flint and fire. That's how Elizabeth and your namesake were."

"Now you've got it, and you'd better not laugh at this skirt," he brooded, standing with his fine-looking strong legs apart, his hands on his hips. "It's for the wedding. And family tradition says that we'll have a proper wedding and you'll get that honeymoon in a bridal tepee. I want more for you than standing up in front of a judge with the Tallchiefs around us. That ceremony served the legal need to make you my wife as fast as I could, but I want you to have everything other Tallchief brides have had. All this was supposed to have been a surprise. Elspeth has been sticking pins and needles in me for a week.''

''Ingrate,'' Elspeth muttered, just as she would to one of her brothers. ''It's a good thing Liam has you to keep him civilized, because I've done my duty with my brothers and husband.''

''Have I told you today that I adore you, lady with dragon-green eyes? Rose of my heart?'' Liam asked in a wary tone.

''Don't try to distract me,'' Michelle said when her mind started rolling again. The sight of Liam with all the Tallchiefs was enough to momentarily take away her breath. He'd come such a long way from the harsh man he'd been, stripped of dreams. Now he spoke of raising calves and plowing and planting and fixing tractors with excitement. He wanted to learn how to ranch on a larger scale, and that would take time. She'd be at his side, every step. Building a home and a ranch and loving Liam were enough excitement to keep her busy for a lifetime. Things had gotten very exciting indeed when she'd put that dent in his pickup fender and ground the straight-stick gears. Liam hadn't ranted, but he'd walked rigidly away from the sight of his beloved truck. Later, working beside him underneath it, he'd been much more pleasant.

An interesting man with neat little edges to explore as the years went by, Liam had kept a secret from her. ''You could have told me about these flints earlier, and you actually used Elizabeth's journal as a guide to understand women.''

Liam shot a glare back at the Tallchief males, who were making smothered chuckling noises. ''I had no other reference for handling a woman like you. I was desperate.''

''You actually read another woman's thoughts to see

how she would react to her beloved, what he did to please her. You used her thoughts for a manual on giving me the things I'd love most. Of serving up those sweet words to stun me. You couldn't just tell me of the legend. Oh, no, you had to make me hunt for it.''

"I gave them to you. They're yours, and so am I.''

Michelle shook her head. "So this is the secret you've been keeping all these weeks. And the legend of the flint and the fire. That's exactly how we are, combustible. I've lost sleep over this, Liam. I've worried that I'd never be able to discover why the flints were wrapped as if they were precious. They were—they were Liam's gift to Elizabeth. You could have told me right away.''

"But then there wouldn't be a game, a challenge for you, would it? At first I didn't believe it myself—that romance and love could come into my life—and then the legend proved true. You responded perfectly…. She's getting wound up,'' Liam murmured in an aside to the Tallchiefs. He tried not to grin, because Michelle's gaze was wandering, warm upon him. From the steamy look of his wife and soon to be his bride again, she loved what she saw. He recognized the warm flush easing up her cheeks, that sultry look beneath her lashes. The flick of her tongue across her lips told him that later she'd be tasting him in a way he loved to return.

He bent to brush his lips upon hers, in the new way he'd discovered to stop her rising temper. Waylaid on the way to scolding him, Michelle whispered, "Your family is right here, Liam.''

"That's right, they are my family, and so are you, lily of my heart.'' Then he wrapped his arms around her and kissed her hungrily. He stepped back to watch her expression. Just the sight of Michelle igniting set off his need to carry her away. Moments later, in the closet next to the kitchen, Michelle's warm mouth parted for his. Her arms locked around him tight, her hands still filled with the flints and the tinderbox. "You'll marry me then, this way?" he asked, uncertain of his appeal while dressed in a skirt.

"I'll take you any way I can get you," she returned against his lips. "We're a family now, boyo. And you're wearing your namesake's ring when we marry. You're quite the romantic, you know."

Liam wrapped his hands in her rippling, silky hair and studied his beloved's heart-shaped face, her meadow-green eyes. She would always look the same to him, years from now—the woman of his body and his soul. His future was here, against him, warm and soft and secure. His past was eons ago, dropping away more every day.

"I didn't think all this was possible," she murmured in the shadows as he caressed her. "I look back at what I was and how much I have now. Sometimes I think it's a dream."

"Dream this," Liam whispered against her lips. After a kiss that spoke of dreams and years together, he started smiling. Then he began to laugh, joy bubbling from him into the tiny shadowy room, echoing in his heart.

"You're beautiful," she said, her hand smoothing his cheek, her eyes adoring him. "And you're blushing. You've come home, then, my love."

"Aye, I have. Home with you."

"Liam? I've noticed that all the Tallchiefs have that same little scar on their thumbs as you have on yours. First I noticed Duncan's, then Calum's and all the rest. Why is that?"

"Accidents, I imagine," he said, and settled back to watch his beloved take the bait. "Nothing to think about."

"No? Why do you have that grin as if you're holding back another secret? I'll find out. You know I will." Then she grabbed him close and kissed him hard, and when they both couldn't breathe, the heat simmering between them, Michelle said, "Aye, I do."

When a man and a woman, equally matched, strike against each other, fire will fly—just like two flints, striking sparks off each other. 'Tis a game, finding the strength of a man and challenging that truth.... For his part, he gave me the two flints, the tinderbox marked with the Tallchief symbol and a love that burns true.

* * * * *

Don't miss Cait London's
next powerful love story,
SLOW FEVER—
the second book in her popular
FREEDOM VALLEY *miniseries—*
on sale December 2000
from Silhouette Desire

And if you want to find out
how the Tallchief saga began, then pick up
the special 3-in-1 Tallchief collection,
A TALLCHIEF CELEBRATION,
featuring the first three stories
in this dynamite series,
available from Silhouette Books
in January 2001.

USA Today Bestselling Author

SHARON SALA

has won readers' hearts with thrilling tales
of romantic suspense. Now Silhouette Books
is proud to present five passionate stories from
this beloved author.

Available in August 2000:
ALWAYS A LADY
A beauty queen whose dreams have been dashed in a
tragic twist of fate seeks shelter for her wounded spirit
in the arms of a rough-edged cowboy....

Available in September 2000:
GENTLE PERSUASION
A brooding detective risks everything to protect the
woman he once let walk away from him....

Available in October 2000:
SARA'S ANGEL
A woman on the run searches desperately for a reclusive
Native American secret agent—the only man who can save
her from the danger that stalks her!

Available in November 2000:
HONOR'S PROMISE
A struggling waitress discovers she is really a rich heiress—
and must enter a powerful new world of wealth and
privilege on the arm of a handsome stranger....

Available in December 2000:
KING'S RANSOM
A lone woman returns home to the ranch where she was
raised, and discovers danger—as well as the man she once
loved with all her heart....

July 2000
BACHELOR DOCTOR
#1303 by Barbara Boswell

August 2000
THE RETURN OF ADAMS CADE
#1309 by BJ James
Men of Belle Terre

September 2000
SLOW WALTZ ACROSS TEXAS
#1315 by Peggy Moreland
Texas Grooms

October 2000
THE DAKOTA MAN
#1321 by Joan Hohl

November 2000
HER PERFECT MAN
#1328 by Mary Lynn Baxter

December 2000
IRRESISTIBLE YOU
#1333 by Barbara Boswell

MAN OF THE MONTH

For twenty years Silhouette has been giving you the ultimate in romantic reads. Come join some of your favorite authors in helping us to celebrate our anniversary with the most rugged, sexy and lovable heroes ever!

Available at your favorite retail outlet.

Silhouette®

Where love comes alive™

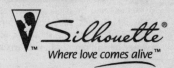

Silhouette®

Desire®

COMING NEXT MONTH

#1315 SLOW WALTZ ACROSS TEXAS—Peggy Moreland
Man of the Month/Texas Grooms
Growing up an orphan had convinced cowboy Clayton Rankin that he didn't need anyone. But when his wife, Rena, told him he was about to lose her, he was determined to win back her love—and have his wife teach him about matters of the heart!

#1316 ROCK SOLID—Jennifer Greene
Body & Soul
She needed to unwind. But when Lexie Woolf saw Cash McKay, relaxation was the last thing on her mind. Cash was everything Lexie had dreamed of in a man—except she feared *she* was not the woman for *him.* Could Cash convince Lexie that their love was rock solid?

#1317 THE NEXT SANTINI BRIDE—Maureen Child
Bachelor Battalion
They were supposed to be together for only one night of passion, but First Sergeant Dan Mahoney couldn't forget Angela Santini. So he set out to seduce the single mom—one tantalizing touch at a time—and convince her that all her nights were meant to be spent with him!

#1318 MAIL-ORDER CINDERELLA—Kathryn Jensen
Fortune's Children: The Grooms
Tyler Fortune needed a bride—and plain librarian Julie Parker fit the bill. But Tyler never counted on falling for his convenient wife. Now he needed to convince Julie that she was the perfect mate for him—so he could become her husband in every way.

#1319 LADY WITH A PAST—Ryanne Corey
She thought no one knew of her former notoriety, but when Connor Garrett tracked down Maxie Calhoon, she had to face her past. Connor stirred emotions in Maxie that she had never experienced, but did he love the woman she once was or the one she had become?

#1320 DOCTOR FOR KEEPS—Kristi Gold
The last thing Dr. Rick Jansen needed was to fall for his new nurse, Miranda Brooks. Yet there was something about Miranda that made it impossible to keep his thoughts—and hands—away from her. But would he still desire Miranda when he learned her secret?